Transit

The Accident Series Book 1

Victoria Traub

CONTENTS

Chapter 1

Darkness. Utter Darkness.

The world is a strange blur of black, with a dizzying, splotchy green. Somewhere in the distance, there are voices. Imperceptible voices.

A light ring begins, followed by low beeps. The world brightens for a moment. A light behind closed eyes.

Then all is quiet.

With a jolt of realization, you open your eyes and suck in a terrified breath.

Where are you? What are you doing in this dark room?

Coughing. The room is saturated with dust.

As you sit up, you become aware that you are on a slab of metal. A table? It quivers with every move you make.

"Hello?" Your voice sounds hollow. Then the table falls apart beneath you. One moment you're moving to get off, the next everything is crashing to the floor in a cacophony of banging metal. Ouch.

What is going on? Where is everyone? Is this some sort of cruel joke?

Wait... What were you doing before you got here? Think! Why can't you just think straight?

zzzzzZZZZZZ Ffft! Beeeuuuuooooo...

A blinding blue light fills the room in harmony with the noises, but then there is a spark and everything fades.

Back to darkness.

"And now we turn to a news update; the U.S. Government has passed a law that will ensure the safety and..." Your last memory; sitting with a group of eager tourists, watching the news fly by on a TV. What happened next? Why is your memory so foggy?

vvVVVVvvv.

Your cell phone buzzes in your back pocket. The screen is dark, but still emanating a light. Nope, it just shut off.

Come on, come on! It won't turn on! Not even to tell you it's run out of battery, it's just... dead.

This is so weird.

Your knee is sore from the crash. Speaking of which; why were you on a weak, rickety table?

Then the lights turn on.

How? You don't know. But one thing is for sure; the room looks like something from a horror movie.

There's only one light bulb, hanging from the ceiling by a thin cord and flickering ominously. The tiled floor is hardly visible through the layer of dirt, and the once white walls are now laced with cobwebs. Over in the far corner are some pretty rusted machines that kind of look like a washer and dryer without the doors. Maybe that's where the blue light came from?

......

"HELP ME!" The words tear from your throat as you scramble to your feet and run over to the wall, banging on it with a fist. As if it's made of soggy paper and not plaster, the small section of wall literally falls apart upon impact and a bright light enters the room, along with a fresh, warm breeze.

What is going on? You reach into the hole and pull the stuff inward, and it all falls down, sending a fury of white dust in the air. Coughing. Swatting away the tendrils of white.

It all settles, revealing the world on the other side.

A jungle. You are in a freaking jungle.

Chapter 2

Now outside, on the quaggy ground. Putting your hands on your head, you turn in a few circles to view the scene in disbelief.

Vines, smooth lumpy trees, leaves, huge blades of grass, and more vines.

The room with the machines is just that; once belonging to a larger building, its outer walls are now jagged and open, much like a rotting carcass. It stands alone in a small clearing, above which the sun is shining hot and bright. What catches your eye most is a bit of paper showing on a piece of wall. Four red letters are visible; *'TINE'*. Circling the building reveals that there were tons of posters once on the wall. They are mostly gone, but one remains in faded letters; *'QUARANTINE'*.

No... Why...? Your heart is pounding when you realized you've clenched your hands into fists.

Your phone still doesn't work.

Then you hear it; the sound of a live engine that grows louder every second.

A vehicle quickly approaching.

You can see it now; a topless Humvee carrying armed soldiers all wearing strange masks.

It reaches the perimeter of the clearing at a terrifying speed and jolts to a stop as the soldiers hop out, all keeping their guns locked on you. You don't register their words and only raise your hands and kneel on the ground in surrender.

Chapter 3

"Who are you?" The soldier at the front speaks, his voice sounding like it's coming through a speaker, "How did you get in a gig without a mask?"

Panic seizes your heart. This has got to be a nightmare. All you manage is a disgruntled, 'uh', and the man smacks you in the jaw with the butt of his gun, sending you to the side. Your mouth drops open and you grip your chin in shock, astounded that the military is allowed to treat civilians this way. The area burns and blood smudges on your hand.

"Speak!" His word sends a jolt through you and you're back on your knees, stammering.

"I don't know! I don't know where I am I just want to go home!"

"What are you flappin' about?" He demands angrily. His eyes dart from you to the building behind you and the open wall.

"I want to go home. To the United States. I don't know how I got here I just want to go back!"

"Are you jagged?" He questions, "There *is* no U.S. Not in a gam." His expressions sound ridiculous, but he says them so passionately you can't help but take him seriously. Before you can ask him what he's saying, another soldier speaks up.

"Cap, probably a NADo. Not first gam we've checked one. Let's just tear."

The soldier who says so is also glancing around nervously, as if expecting something to pounce on them at any moment.

The first soldier (obviously their captain) speaks again, but not to you.

"Yeah, you're right." He pulls something from his belt that looks like a scanner and places it on your forehead.

Beep, beep, beep.

"All clear." He removes the scanner and nudges his gun at you, "No gamming, you'll get bagged at the Safe Zone. For now, just sit tight and shut your flapper."

When you stand to your feet he continuously nudges you toward the Humvee until you're climbing in. A rise of panic. Something tells you this building and the machines are an important key to what happened to you. You don't want to leave them! But it's the military; you have to obey them. Besides; you must be in a war zone or something.

A war zone...

All of the soldiers back up to the vehicle with their guns pointed out and sweeping back and forth around the clearing. What are they scared of? What is happening!?!

When you're situated on the floor, the captain spins a pointed finger in the air in signal to the others saying, "Let's tear out!"

Chapter 4

The vehicle begins moving.

Towards the quarantine room at first, but then it turns in a tight circle and bolts into action, crashing through the jungle at an insanely fast speed. You briefly catch sight of the speedometer and see that it is traveling around 80 mph.

One of the soldiers holds out a mask that looks like theirs.

Filter. The word punches you in the face. You snatch the mask and slide it over your head.

Whrrrrr, scchhhllp.

You feel it suction around your nose and jaw and a high-pitched squeal sounds. Fresh air. You cannot deny that it is amazing after the stifling room and warm, moist jungle air.

"How did you shiv this long without gigs?"

Is the soldier talking to you? Yep, yes he is.

You imagine his face being full of wonder, though you can only see his eyes behind the clear plastic that serves as his visor. He looks away, knowing you won't say anything.

It is now that you notice the other soldiers are crouched along the perimeter of the vehicle, with their guns aimed at the outside world. What are they aiming at?

The same soldier from before glances down at your movement and puts a harsh hand on your shoulder to steady you as the vehicle runs over a bump and you lift from your seat. You'd almost dove overboard into the thick of the looming jungle.

"Easy." He calls out, "Best not move on this gig unless you get it. You'd better catch a charge; you seem pretty digged out." When you don't move, he leans over and shoves you on the ground.

Dude!

"Go to charging!" He orders, but you only stare at him. His eyes squint in confusion, "You don't get what I said, do you?"

Finally. You shake your head and he flinches in surprise.

"Now that's a first. I told you to charge. You know, charge...?" He tilts his head to the side and closes his eyes, but it still makes no sense. He grabs the soldier next to him, "Hey jag, what's the word they used for charging?"

The other guy's voice, regardless of the mask, sounds more mature. Without pulling his eyes away from the sight of his gun, he replies,

"You mean sleeping, you trip?"

The first soldier gives him a harsh pat.

"That's it!" He looks at you again, "Go to sleeping."

He doesn't know what sleeping is? Maybe he's foreign? But he has no accent.

... How can you sleep right now? This makes no sense!

Just lay down and hope they leave you alone.

Sliding to the hard, metal floor and curling up with your back against the side, you think about the last few minutes of your life. The confusion and panic are almost too much to bear.

Someone hastily throws a rough, itchy blanket on you, but you cannot sleep. Not with the questions and the fear and the endless jostling of the Humvee. Where is everyone? They are probably so worried about you, to find that you've gone missing and are nowhere to be found. But where are *you*?

Chapter 5

Slowing down, slowing way down.

It's been hours since you were picked up and this is the first time the vehicle has stopped. What's going on?

"We're just shooting up some gas." Your soldier friend explains, but his words mean nothing until you see what he's referring to; a pipe coming from the ground and several knobs on the side with a thick tube rolled and hanging on a hook.

"You never checked one before, have you?" He points out. You cannot take your eyes away from the strange pipe and make no reply. What is he even saying?

"*Dan*," he replies emphatically, "NADo must have shot you jamming flat."

"What is NADo?" It sounds weird coming from you, as if you are saying a bad word. He scoffs and his breath fogs up the lower half of his visor.

"Neurological Amnesia Disorder. The *Tornado's*...?" He responds questioningly, "You feel them inside you, right?"

"... No."

"Check it. Don't know why I even asked; most of you don't get jack anyways. Though you're the first that doesn't seem completely jammed. Still, there are some that don't shoot up and only act like nothing's ever happened – like you."

"Well, what are they?" You ask and he falls silent, evidently saying too much already, "Just tell me." You plead, "Where am I? Why was I in a quarantined room? What did that scanner do? What are the tornados – what does that pipe do?"

The soldier holds up his hands defensively,

"Whoa, slow down. They only jam it up when you try to get things. Meds at the Safe Zone will bag you, if they can."

Your mouth falls open slightly in disbelief. You know the military has their own slang, but this just makes no sense. Everything he says sounds horrible and confusing. The soldier sighs.

"Check it; we're told not to bag a NADo – could jam them flat – but you seem tougher than the others. Weird, because NADo's are usually wusses. Anyways; *that*," he nods his head towards the pipe that the captain is hooking up to the Humvee, "is a gas pipe. We're shooting up before we continue. Won't make it to the Safe Zone if we don't."

A gas pipe. Leaning to the side of the Humvee, you now see that the captain has the pipe hooked up to a filler tube. The soft whir of flowing gas can be heard.

You should be happy at learning something, but the answer only makes you hungry for more.

"Where am I?" You ask next.

"Can't tell you that much. That's up to the Meds."

"I don't think I am whatever you think I am... a NADo? The last I knew I was..."

"Stop right there," he interrupts, "That's your problem. Getting the last bit of normal life before. That's what all NADo's flap about. Can't seem to get their digs to accept reality, and how jagged it really is."

"Heh!" Scoffs another soldier, "The -"

He goes off and starts swearing at his miserable life. You're not sure why it is shocking, you've heard swearing before. The nicer soldier jabs his gun into the stomach of the other soldier.

"Dug, you shot? You know we're not supposed to cuss in front of Civ's." He says. The other soldier pounds his fist into your friend's arm.

"Who jamming gives a shot?" He argues, but your friend turns in his seat to face the soldier directly.

"You want to get jammed? Cause that's what it'll get you if you don't flap up right now."

The captain interrupts them by clanging his gun against the Humvee.

"Flap it, all of you! You wanna get us killed?"

Oh, no! You are supposed to be quiet? You glance around, expecting to see a sinister enemy soldier with a sniper aimed right at you.

"Doesn't matter." Someone replies, "The jammed things will come anyways and there's nothing sound can do about it."

... *Things*? They aren't talking about enemy soldiers? The guy's comment sounds like they are talking about animals. Maybe there are lions or jaguars? Wait, no; lions don't actually live in jungles. Even still.

"Wh-what things?" Your voice comes out weaker than you intended, and you imagine them all smiling at you, like they are about to tell a ghost story. As if on cue, a loud roar echoes through the jungle, the only animal noise you've heard since coming out of the room.

Chapter 6

It sounds like a strange bird crossed with a baboon and a dying woman. You feel your face become pale as you look around. That certainly is not the roar of a wild cat. Your pulse has quickened to an alarming rate. Your eyes catch one of the soldier's and he shoves his thumb over his shoulder.

"Those things." He says with a snicker.

Thunk.

The tank is full, and the captain rolls up the tube and sets it back on the pipe.

"Let's tear!" He screams as he climbs back into the vehicle and racks his gun, "Eyes on anything that moves."

You don't notice who starts the vehicle, only feel its wheels begin turning as it lolls forward. You sit facing the jungle and your hands grip the sides of the Humvee until your knuckles are white.

The jungle is a haze of shadows. Then the soldiers turn on flashlights attached to their guns and the foliage is illuminated in several white spots. A little to your right, the brush begins shaking, but a soldier has already aimed his gun and released several bullets into the thing before you can see what it is.

Then the vehicle takes off in a shot. Shouts to your left alert you and you turn to see something they are shooting at standing in the path of the vehicle.

KA – thump. Crunch.

The vehicle does not stop and just plows right over it.

Click, click, click.

The soldier next to you is shoving several cartridges into the chamber.

"Jammed vintage gigs." He complains, "Wish they'd give us better sups instead of forcing us to use antiques like we don't jam our digs protecting their precious tanks." When he finishes reloading, he racks it and aims it back out into the jungle.

Something about his words fills you with despair and you sink back to the ground instead of trying to see what they are shooting at. Doubt it would be possible anyways, with

P a g e | 24

how fast you are now moving and how trained the soldiers are.

At least you are safe.

Except for what he implied about the vintage guns... which is weird, since they look pretty normal to you.

Exhaling a harsh sigh, you bring your knees up and sit with your head in your hands until the firing stops and all that can be heard is the whirring of the wheels and heavy engine. Then you are overwhelmed by sleep.

Chapter 7

You have a weird dream. You're being escorted by soldiers into an old house. They don't have masks, but they are all wearing nerdy glasses.

"Get to the room! Now!"

Who is shouting? His voice is so obnoxious. The scene is foggy looking, as if you are looking at everyone from squinted eyes. Where are they taking you? For some reason, you are aware that you are not standing up. But you should be. Weren't they just escorting you? No. You are lying flat on your back on a metal table that they are now wheeling through the front door. Your eyes open more to see that the interior of the house looks like a hospital.

This shouldn't be happening. The more you try to stand, the heavier you feel. Panicked. Why won't your body obey you? Something itches at the back of your mind, telling you it's a dream.

Get up! Get up! You scream in your head. Then your body begins jerking up, as if trying to sit up but being held down by some unseen force.

Awake. Sitting up, looking around. You are not in the jungle anymore.

Above you, the sky is dark and cloudless, littered with stars. It's terribly cold. The soldiers are all asleep. The back of your head hurts; you must have banged it on the floor.

Wait, no one's driving the vehicle!

… Oh. Duh; the whole thing is self operational. There is not even a steering wheel.

Huh. The dashboard is at the rear. That's weird. It kind of seems like you're driving backwards. You glance at the speed. It's slowed down to 40 mph.

You are now in a vast desert, with no land in sight in any direction. It's weird, sitting there, feeling the wheels glide across the soft sand and the soldiers all asleep. It feels vulnerable and yet you must be safe or else the others would not be sleeping.

Eyes becoming heavy with tiredness. Blinking into a sleep.

Is that a man…? Snap, there's a man in the distance. On top a sand dune.

Electricity flows through you and you are wide awake.

He's too far away to see details, but something about him is odd. He's just standing there, slightly hunched over, watching your vehicle pass – not even waving his hands or calling for help. How can he survive in a desert with no land in sight?

Once your initial shock wears off, you grab the soldier next to you and shake him awake. He sits up with alert, but seems annoyed.

"What are you jagging?" He demands.

"Shouldn't we help that man?" You ask and point at the stranger. The soldier follows your gaze and then laughs. He brings the site of his gun to his face and snipes the man.

POW

The explosion of his gun echoes across the desert. None of the other soldiers even stir, as if they are used to random shots being fired in their sleep.

At the same time, the vehicle lurches and picks up speed, accelerating to 120 mph.

You are shocked. When he'd fired, you grabbed your head and watched the strangers body twist awkwardly from the impact.

He falls, tumbling down the dune like a dummy.

"Go back to charging." The soldier murmurs, "They won't jam us out here."

The soldier casually sits back down and his head falls limp as he goes to sleep again.

Your heart is pounding. It was so much louder than you thought it would be. How'd he get a sniper rifle anyways? Where'd it come from?

When you look back at where the stranger fell, you are astounded to see that he's gone.

Perhaps it's just an optical illusion. Like, maybe there's a dune in the way and you just can't see it. But you know that's not true; you can still see the blood in the sand and the imprints he left from his fall. There are also snaking footprints, like he stood and dragged himself away and out of sight.

So that's it then? They are just going to leave a helpless man to survive alone in a desert, with nothing but a bloody gunshot wound? It's almost worse than just killing him. What is going on?

Chapter 8

You jolt awake at the first harsh bump.

The entire vehicle is shaking and rumbling, like it's driving over rough ground. The sun is glaring overhead and you quickly realize you are the only one still asleep and so you sit up.

Still in the desert. But the ground is now flat and dry, with small boulders littering it. In front of you is a huge, cracked cement wall topped with some sort of bright material that reflects the sun in a deadly shine. The vehicle slows the closer it gets.

A large, rusted metal door opens in the side and you pass through into a long corridor. When the soldiers all hop off the vehicle, you do too and you follow them as they begin walking forward. The Humvee disappears into another doorway, behind which other vehicles are parked.

Covering the top of the facility, is some sort of unpromising clear plastic that's haphazardly taped together at the seams. The slightest wind sends a snaking ripple across it. So that's what the weird shiny stuff is.

A hissing noise distracts you and you are soon surrounded in a white fog. A moment later, it's gone. The pressure in the room increases as the air sucks out. Oddly enough, your only thought is on the plastic. It's pulled taught and just as it seems like it might burst open, it springs upward in a loose wave. The cleansing was so quick, you did not initially realize it took away your breath for a moment.

Ahead, the soldiers are pulling off their masks and you do too. Their physiques range from mid-twenties to late thirties, but you can't tell which one had been which. Though they vary in looks, they all have similar heights. The oldest has dark scruffy facial hair and you assume he's the captain.

When you all reach the end of the corridor, another door opens and the inside is quiet and empty except for one large, windowless building.

The captain speaks now, and his voice is gruff but soft.

"Max, you're tagged." Is all he says. A blond guy comes up next to you with his gun in his hands, preparing to escort you somewhere. The others walk off together in a group and you are left alone with the soldier. You wonder if he is the one who was being nice to you earlier. Feeling a sense of awkwardness in the air, you try to break it.

"Max...?" You question. He only smirks.

"This way." He says and begins walking. Though their live voices are impossible to compare to the mechanics of the mask, you somehow know this isn't the same guy. His sounds lazy and his words are slurred, like he doesn't care at all what happens.

He takes you into the building. The people crossing your path wear scrubs or uniforms, carrying clipboards and cellular devices that squeal with a chalky voice on the other end spewing out information. Sometimes a woman's voice comes over a speaker, requesting for a specific individual to report to the operations unit. Whatever that means.

You follow the soldier down different hallways and up a flight of stairs. The whole thing is bizarre; it is a perfectly functional facility, but the walls and floors are made of cement with no decorations or signs. The only consolation you have is the occasional gust of cool air blowing from an air vent. The rest looks dreary and desperate, like someone made the building in a hurry.

Finally, you are brought to what you assume is a medical center because of the concentration of people in scrubs rolling around wooden carts of bottles, machinery, and instruments. He brings you to a group of women who are standing in a circle. Some of them are holding clipboards and they seemed to have been talking about something important until your escort walked up.

"Is Jenny in?" He questions and they all break out in giddy grins. One in particular reaches for a wireless phone clipped to her waist.

"Yeah, let me page her." She says with a smile and pushes on a button, "Jenny, your dug is here with another Civ."

You feel embarrassed for him as they will not stop giggling and making jokes. His face is bright red by the time, 'Jenny' comes. She is a younger woman with straight, light brown hair and soft blue eyes. She also is dressed in scrubs and has a white T-shirt underneath with the sleeves pulled up to her elbows and a black wristwatch on one arm. When they see each other, they embrace in a quick hug that you detect a lot of emotion beneath. You can see the worry they have in their eyes, but they are trying to remain professional.

"What, you didn't bring me any flowers?" She jokes. You don't know why what she said is funny, but everyone chuckles at it. The soldier does his quirky smirk again and nods his head towards you.

"Found this dug 50 miles from the gigs. A NADo. We need to bag em' before we flip em' to the Tank." He explains and Jenny nods.

… Are they planning to kill you? You suddenly have a weird sensation like maybe you should run for it.

"Checked, follow me." She turns and begins walking and the soldier nudges you forward with the barrel of his gun. Nope.

Your heart is pounding, but you bolt into action and charge back the way you came, sprinting as fast as you can possibly go.

Chapter 9

Where to go? Do you even remember the way out?

Everyone shoots you strange looks as you zoom by.

You just *cannot* be bagged and flipped to some tank!

But you are in a military facility in the middle of a desert. You won't survive out there. You'll probably die anyways.

The thought slows you down for just a moment. Enough to close the distance between you and the pursuing soldier. The next thing you know, you're crashing to the ground. Your chin smacks into the concrete, and your arms are yanked behind you in an agonizing twist.

"NO!" You scream, "Don't kill me! Let me GO!"

In your panic, you don't see the nurse walk up with a syringe. All you feel is a prick and the entrance of liquids into your system and your mind fogs over. Nope. You've blacked out.

Awake again. You're on a cot in a small white room with a plain white door with nothing but a square window. The rest of the room is empty. Wait... No; there's another cot to your left and on it is a girl a little older than you. Her visage scares you because it is so... tired looking. Her hair is jaggedly cut to a short length, she is deathly skinny, and her eyes are sunken in and grey. She looks like she hasn't slept in ages.

Sitting up. Oof. Your head hurts so bad. And your chin! You touch it gingerly, surprised that it's not bandaged or scabbed. It's only numb.

You are in a one pieced suit and a jacket that is like a zip up hoodie, but made of military material on the outside and soft, synthetic material on the inside. You feel impeccably clean. The combat boots are your size and there is also a belt, with pouches and clips. On your arm is a white number stitched onto the bicep; '18'.

On your wrist is a hospital bracelet, and you snatch it and twist it to read it.

'Patient: J. Jack. Sterilization: Complete. Diagnosis: No impending diseases or disorders. Status: Ready to be deployed.'

Relief washes through you. Surely if you were a NADo it would have said. And being deployed certainly sounds better than being bagged. Something else catches your attention. A date at the bottom; *'Day: 136 Year: 2100'*

Chapter 10

Whaaaaaat on earth?

2100? How is that possible? Does it really say 2100? Yes. It does. Oh! Duh. It's obviously a typo and is supposed to say, *2020*. Few! That was weird.

Looking around the room again.

Your cell mate, (cell mate? Is this a prison?) is sitting on her bed with her back against the wall. She is also in military clothing.

The walls are bare and from what you can see, there appear to be no cameras or speakers, but you doubt that's really the case. There are no lights, but the room is somehow illuminated in fluorescent brightness.

You look back at the girl, who is staring at the floor with a blank expression on her face.

"Hey." You call out, and she doesn't move. "Why are we here?"

"We're waiting, obviously." The response surprises you.

"For what? What are they going to do to us?" You press.

"Doesn't it say on your bracelet?" She retorts in a condescending tone. Ok. Yeah, you could easily guess you were being deployed, but to where?

"What's your name?" You ask instead. She scoffs and shakes her head. Her next words are heavy with sarcasm,

"Avery Darr. Sterilization: Complete. Diagnosis: No impending diseases or disorders. Status: Ready to be deployed."

"Why does my bracelet say, Patient: J. Jack?" You ask. For some reason, the girl looks up at you now, a look of complete disgust on her face.

"What, I get to share a gig with a jagging NADo? I thought they could bag that."

You feel a surge of anger and frustration at these weird terms. How do you even answer something like that?

"What even is a NADo?" You reply, not sure if NADo even *is* a disease or disorder.

"Then why are you so jammed? How do you not get anything?"

...

"I don't know. I woke up in a room and soldiers showed up and arrested me."

"Oh." She kind of rolls her eyes around as if she's not sure what to say next, "Um, J. Jack means Juvenile Jack. It means you are younger than twenty and they don't know who you are. Explains why they rolled you in here on a cot and unconscious."

"Can you tell me what's going on?" You ask flatly.

"We're being, 'rescued' and flipped to the City – man I hate jammed questions." She stirs in annoyance when she says the last part.

"The City? Rescued from what? What is going on out there?" The questions do not stop pounding your head; like a jackhammer digging a hole into the very center of your nervous system.

"Wow. You really don't know jack, do you? You basically are a NADo." Her voice is husky, as if she spends a lot of time screaming.

"I guess so. I don't even know what a NADo is. No one will explain anything." But you can tell that Avery certainly does not want to be the one to explain.

"Well, what do you get? What's your name and what do you do?" She questions.

"What do you mean, 'what do I do?' I'm not even graduated from high school!"

She stares at you with confused eyes.

"You don't flap a check." She says. "They did a psych check on you, right?"

Ouch.

"I'm not crazy!" You reply, "I'm from America and the date was March 15th, 2020 a few days ago. I was touring a science facility in Alaska. That's the last I knew. A crazy person couldn't tell you that stuff."

Avery is not convinced.

"2020!" She laughs, "They say that crazies don't get that they are. You're definitely crazy if you get it's 2020. You probably jammed that into your brain when you're mom died or something - 2020 is when the Accident happened."

What does she mean?

"But..." You fight, "I *know* what I'm talking about!"

"No wonder they jammed you up earlier." She murmurs.

"Fine. What is today's date?" You ask.

"What does that mean?"

Argh!

"What year is it?"

"2100, obviously." She shakes her head when she says so, as if you're so dumb for not knowing.

Standing up, you head over to the door and go to pound your fist on it, but it slides open with a hiss the moment you're in front of it.

Chapter 11

The hallway outside the room is a part of the facility. You can tell by the cement ceiling, walls, and floor. White doors break the plainness every twenty feet or so, obviously more rooms like yours. There are no lights, and you realize there never have been, only a few bright lamps stuck here and there, but this hallway is in darkness.

What were you expecting to see? A bunch of people in scrubs like before, a nurse maybe or even a cleaning lady? You could run for it.

Avery breaks your thoughts.

"Don't be jammed. It's night, no one is out there right now. We're supposed to be charging ourselves."

"So this isn't a prison?"

"Hah!" She scoffs, "If it was, I would commit the worst crime if it meant getting me indoors."

"Why, what makes it so bad out there?"

"Besides the jammed air? You need a mask. Without one there is no jag to anything. Then you need a gig. Those two things are probably more important than food and water."

"What's a gig?" Your question sends a wave of confusion across her face.

"Your memory loss make you forget how to flap?" She spits.

"What's a flap?" You press, feeling that surge of frustration again. Avery stares at you hard, her thoughts unreadable.

"A flap is a dan mouth. I asked you if you forgot how to speak, which you apparently have. A gig is a useful jag. It can mean anything; a base, a Humvee, a jam. I just said you need a mask and a jam."

This makes no sense!

"What is a jam?"

"How do I answer *that*?" She questions, eyes narrowed, "A jam! You know:" She holds her hands up as if she's holding a gun. Your mind reverts to the time the soldier was searching for the word *sleep*.

"You mean a gun?" You respond and she looks even more confused.

"What are you talking about?"

Before you can press, the light in your room shuts off. You hear Avery again,

"I guess they want us to go to charging."

You bury your face in your hands. This is so unbelievable. It's just, *not* happening! It can't be happening! You have to talk to someone who actually knows what's going on!

A series of rustling noises appear and you know Avery is crawling under the covers of her cot. This is absolutely insane.

Fumbling around in the dark, you find your cot and crawl onto it, sitting where the bed meets the wall and hugging the sheets up to your chest. As your eyes adjust, you can see that the hallway outside your room is slightly lighter, making the window a spot of gray. Occasionally, a noise echoes somewhere in the facility, but silence mostly eats up the minutes.

Eighty years. That can't be. This can't be happening.

Chapter 12

Minutes stretch into hours, and still you are awake. Sleeping just seems like a dumb thing to do. Assuming it was 8:00 pm when the lights shut off, (probably more like 9:00) you've been sitting here for over 6 hours for sure, not counting the times you dozed off. That puts you anywhere between 2:00 am to 4:00 am.

Noises start appearing. Sounds of people waking, carts rolling around, lights in the hallway turn on. Then your room illuminates in that weird fluorescent light. Ouch it's bright. Why are people up so early?

Avery stirs and sits up sleepily, staring at the door with an edge of suspicion. It's now that you notice she has a backpack next to her bed. Do you? Yes! You do! What's in it?

The material is lightweight and scratchy. Inside are a few packages of some sort of purple jelly, and your cell phone. Nope, still doesn't work. There's a watch. It's 6:00 in the morning.

Woah that's way different than your calculation.

Something in the room starts hissing. Two holes open and out of them shoot metal trays, one for each person. On each is a water bottle and a container with what looks like baby food pooled inside. It smells like baby food too.

You are disgusted at first, until you see Avery shoving it down as if it's the most delicious meal ever.

You *are* really hungry too. How many days has it been since you've eaten? You decide you should tough it up and so you grab the food and begin eating almost as fiercely as Avery.

It is bland. Really bland. But you are thankful to feel a full stomach when it's all gone.

"You know," you look up to see Avery taking sips of water as she's speaking, "you'd better start jamming like you know what's checked. I'd stop using those words too; make you sound jagged. You'll learn a lot more that way, instead of flapping up."

"Thanks." You reply. "... How," you stop in mid-sentence, not quite sure what you're saying, "How do things work?"

"Like the government?" She replies questioningly.

You nod.

"There's not much to tell." She says, "There's just one 'perfect' city with one digged government and 365 days that are used for records." The way she talks about this city gives you the impression she's either mocking it or loathing it. Maybe both.

"Where are we?"

"In a Sterilization Facility."

"No, I mean where is it? Where is this place? Aren't we in America?"

"What is Umeruga? Is that a Supplier?"

"You blame me of not knowing anything and yet you don't know anything about real life! Am I in some sort of science experiment? If so, that's illegal. And I'm going to sue whoever is behind it."

Avery scoffs, "They shouldn't be sending you to the City in this state. You're supposed to be checked before being transitioned."

"I've heard the City mentioned several times now. Is it like a safe haven or something?"

She laughs and shakes her head, confirming your suspicions about the loathing. Her nose twitches almost like a snarl for a moment, but then she stares up at the ceiling in thought,

"You'll check it. I can't explain it to you since you've lost your dan brain. I've never been there myself. Spent the last twenty years of my jagged life trying to shiv in this flat."

You stare at her with surprise, but she starts playing with something in her hands. You are about to ask her what it is, but the door opens with a hiss and a soldier comes in, carrying a clipboard. He looks at both of you and then down at the papers.

"... J. Jack and Avery Darr?" He questions.

"That's us." Avery casually agrees and stands up from the bed expectantly. You follow suit. The soldier tucks the papers under his arm.

"Get your gigs and follow me."

Avery snags her backpack off the ground and zooms out the door into the hallway. The soldier looks at you expectantly. So, you grab your backpack and do the same.

Chapter 13

The soldier brings you to a steamy, hot place that is evidently where people take showers. There are other rooms in the midst of it, and you realize it's more like a locker room than showers. There is one hallway lined with doors and he first stops there and tells the both of you to, "empty your contents". Turns out it's just bathrooms.

The soldier is waiting outside the locker rooms and when you all meet up, he continues to guide you through the facility. It seems impossible to determine how the rooms fit together or which direction they are going or how the different units are lined up. There are no signs or anything to indicate locations. How do the workers remember? They spend all of their time there, moving people from unit to unit, so they probably have it memorized.

An elevator. Ah, something familiar at last. Except, it is made of a metal grate that squeals threateningly with each move. A doorway to each floor zooms by as you fall to ground level.

At the bottom, the door screeches open. On the other side are the main hallways you entered through. There are a lot of people , identifiable as soldiers, doctors, nurses, or clerks. So this is mainly a medical facility. But a military medical facility. You shake your head; it hurts trying to figure out what it is and how things work.

The soldier steps out and walks down the length, with you and Avery following closely at his heels. Once you are a few feet away from the doors, something beeps and the doors open automatically and a gust of cool air blows in. It feels artificial, and you remember that you are still inside the walls with the clear plastic roof.

Chapter 14

The ground outside is desert-ish with a soft crunch beneath your feet. The soldier leads you across its width to the wall, to a very specific location, and a hole opens up like a doorway.

Inside, other passengers are waiting. A slight murmur fills the air and glances are cast your way when you enter. Standing next to the group, is a truck similar to the Humvee except it is bigger. That also means, though, that it will travel at a slower speed and will need more gas.

The room is dark; the only light is from an orange bulb and the open door. A few seconds later, it shuts and you are all left to the dull glow of the bulb.

There are no women in the group, only males. Everyone is dressed in the same attire except the soldiers. They have military clothing that looks heavier and baggier, with tons of pockets and straps and belts that are fraying and dusty looking. This group is a lot older, except for one guy who is quiet and has dark brown hair. He's wearing a nerdy pair of spectacles. Hah! What a nerd. How is he a soldier?

The door opens and another pair of civilians is escorted by a soldier.

Max, the blond soldier who tackled you earlier. He stands tensely and has a scowl on his face that says he does not want to be there, and occasionally he shoots you a suspicious look.

Your heart begins racing; this type of attention is dangerous in an era like this. You don't know why, but blending in seems so much better than being flagged and babysat.

"Check it, listen up!" Another soldier comes from the darkness, probably the captain, and he is shouting to get everyone's attention, "Do exactly as we say and stay in the gig unless otherwise commanded. Each of you will be given a jam that only fires when it checks Kroko-dillies, so don't even think about tryin' to flat anything else." Several people snicker at this. Why do they only want to shoot at crocodiles? Maybe they are planning to travel through swamps. Does that mean you are going through the southern states? But even so, there are mostly alligators, not crocodiles, in the U.S.

The soldier is still speaking.

"... daily rations are already in your gigs, so don't be asking us for food. Takes four days to get to the City from here and as you all know, haste is mandatory for shiving. You'll all get masks, but don't take them off unless you wanna die. Meaning exactly that; we will flat you if you take them off. Easier than you going Krok on us."

You scratch your forehead; their conversation is so weird. But Avery said to pretend like you know what's going on.

"Numbers are on your jackets; easier than learning names. Now climb aboard and grab your gigs!"

Chapter 15

You climb into the truck after everyone else, to the corner closest to the front on a spot that has a big '18' sticker on it. On each seat is a mask, a strange looking gun, and a water bottle fitted inside a body strap. The gun is black, with elaborate workings and contraptions. How do they expect anyone to use them? Surely no one knows how they work except the soldiers.

You follow when the civilians fasten the water bottle around their body. The strap is squishy and there's a spout coming off of it. Must be extra water stored inside. You almost put the mask on, but see that no one else is doing so and instead, you just hold it and sling your gun over your shoulder.

The other passengers all look terrified. If only you knew where you are and what is going on, maybe you'd understand why.

"You check like a flier." Avery whispers to you. Your first instinct is to ask her what she means, but you stop. Just think about it for a moment: you. check. like. a. flier. Nope: still doesn't make sense.

"I don't know," you say back, "I don't mean to."
Hopefully that response is appropriate.

Avery chuckles,

"Well, if you've shived this far, then you're probably
digging instincts. Dan it; you are ready to flip, and yet you
don't get how jagged it actually is. Of course," she shifts in her
seat and starts messing with the workings of her gun, "we
have a small army of Rips, so I don't know why I am scared."
She kind of laughs nervously. She's scared.

"... Who is Dan?"

Her eyes grow big and she looks at you with her jaw
dropped.

"You're jagged." Is all she says.

Take a deep breath.

The captain climbs in last and pushes a couple of
buttons on the dashboard and it revs to life. There's
movement above you. It's a barely visible line that passes
over the truck. When it reaches the dashboard, a popping and
hissing noise sounds as if something is sealing shut.

Maybe it is a roof. Nope; your hand only hits air.

Avery notices your actions and leans in to speak.

"It's just to block out the wind." She says.

"It doesn't block out anything else? Like bullets?"

She gives you a weird look and then laughs slightly,

"Yeah, you wish the jags in the City would shoot enough to give us tech like that."

The headlights of the vehicle click on in both directions and more of the room is illuminated. It is a large hangar, lined with tons of different military vehicles, and a few planes.

"Why don't we just fly there?" You blurt, and everyone snickers and shakes their heads, except the nerdy guy. He stares at you with a concerned furrow. Avery digs her heel into your boot and hisses,

"Flap it!"

You blush and look away in silence. It was a smart question; why did people reacted that way?

Another door opens in the side of the hangar, and you come out into a corridor like the one you entered through before. Everyone slips on their masks and you do too, feeling the air suction out of the room like before. Only this time, the doors at the end open and a gust of hot, dusty air comes rushing in to meet you.

Chapter 16

The mask churns with electronics, and then you start the in and out wheezes of filtered air. You can hear everyone else breathing through the system as well.

The outside world is still desert. Nothing has changed. The sky is cloudless and the sun glints off the golden earth with a hateful burning. In one moment, the vehicle picks up speed and is pounding across the bumpy ground, kicking up a cloud of dust behind.

Now that everyone has their masks on, it is impossible to differentiate them except for their numbers. The fact that the soldiers have numbers too must be an invitation for the civilians to talk to them, but it just seems like a dumb thing to.

A couple miles into the trip you come to a large gate that goes to the right and left for miles. When the Humvee reaches it, it squeals and rolls back automatically, letting you pass through to the outside world. Once through, it closes again and you are no longer in its protection.

With the sun glaring overhead, it is unbearably hot. After the first hour, you are drenched in sweat and your mask is fogging up. Don't take your jacket off though, because none of the others do. How on earth they can handle this heat?

Avery suddenly grabs your arm and pulls back a patch of cloth that was previously covering up a keypad and punches something into it. Immediately, the inside of your jacket becomes wonderfully cold.

Mountains are forming along the horizon. By evening, you've reached them. They are dry, with bare bushes peeking through the cracks, and the rock is a tan color that looks orange against the evening sky.

You drive through these rocks well into the night. No one sleeps as the mountains are creepy looking. There are too many shadows and too many crevices for things to hide in.

Then the vehicle slows to a stop.

"Dig break." The captain calls and hops out of the vehicle. Several others follow, but you remain seated, as does Avery. Seems like a great idea to wander off in the dark, in a maze of sinister rocks with no idea what to expect.

The remainder of you are silent. Then you hear scuffling feet approaching and everyone stands.

Click, click, click, click, click.

They start triggering the thing.

It's the captain, but everyone is firing at him like he's some sort of garbled demon. He doesn't miss a beat.

"Stop it you jagged trips. It's just me." He exclaims and gradually the empty ticks stop. He climbs onto the vehicle and makes his way to the back, "If the others don't show up in three minutes, we're flipping without them."

So, these tough people are trigger happy; that means they are more scared than they let on. What's more; you are the only civilian who didn't jump to their feet and go berserk on the captain, which means you are more suspicious than ever.

Well, shoot. Pretending to be like everyone else is proving more and more difficult.

Thank goodness the others are returning now, but everyone stops dead in their tracks. Your blood becomes icy and you freeze in your seat.

It is a roar, just like the one from the jungle, only this time it bounces off the rocks and shatters your bones. This time it does not sound like an animal, it sounds purely human, like some loony is hanging out in the rocks and shrieking at the top of his lungs.

The other's bolt to the truck and hop in, heading to their seats as quickly as possible. The captain starts up the truck and it rolls forward.

"Gam it, let's tear!" He shouts. No one prepares to shoot at things like they'd done in the jungle, and so it's probably safe. Scooting forward and onto the ground with your back against the bench.

Chapter 17

Avery shakes you awake in the morning. Still in the mountains.

"Gamming food." She tells you. What? She's wiggling a packet of that weird jelly stuff in your face. Food.

"I'm not hungry." You reply, to which Avery asks,

"Trying to flat yourself? You don't have the luxury out here. Takes a long time to die of starvation, and if we run into any danger, you'll want your strength. Trust me." With that, she pulls some sort of straw from her mask, sticks it in the packet, and starts slurping up the jelly.

You sigh and go to rub your face, but remember the mask, and instead sit up on the bench. Your jacket is deathly cold now that it's morning. How did you sleep with it like that? How can you turn it off? It was under this flap of cloth on your sleeve. There are little buttons and a screen showing the temperature at 68°. Avery stops you.

"Don't do that." She says, "It still gets jagged in the rocks and you'll want it to be cold when the sun gams."

Instead of responding, you open up your backpack and bring out your own jelly. It is made of fruit, but tastes like it's been injected with supplements. It has that tangy, vitamin, oily taste that makes your tongue sour. Hey; you forgot about your phone! You pull it out and hold down the power button. Still dead. Why did you even bother to check?

"Where did you get that!?!" Avery's words make you jump in your seat.

"Can you maybe not scream in my ear?" You say, but she's not looking at you. She's staring at the phone with wide eyes. She suddenly snatches it and starts looking at it all over.

"Hey, give it back!" You reach out but she turns her back to you.

"Hah! This is jagged. I can't get you have one! It checks new! You get how much these are worth, right?"

Finally, you take it from her and shove it into the neckline of your jumpsuit. "Hey!" Avery says, "Let me check it for a gam!"

"Dude, just shut up already." You hiss, "I don't want other people knowing I have one."

She glances around,

"Sorry, I just... I've only ever heard of them. Never checked one myself. A... tel, telli, telli-something?"

"A cell phone."

"Where did you get it?" She asks.

"Technically, I bought it. But since we're all pretending like nothing normal exists, it was on me when they picked me up." You explain.

She nudges you.

"I bet we can find someone in the City who can bag it."

"No! Why would I want someone to do that?" You exclaim. She rolls her eyes.

"So it can work, you trip? Dan, you're so jammed. Why would you not want someone to bag it?"

... Bag means fix! *'meds at the safe zone will* bag *you.'* *'we have to* bag *em' and flip em' to the Tank.'* That's why they freaked when you ran off.

"Oh!" You laugh nervously, "I thought you said something else. Of course I want it... bagged."

Avery laughs at you.

"You're so jammed." She says.

Chapter 18

Driving, eating, adjusting your jackets, another bathroom break. This time you go, while it's still morning. Regardless of the sunlight though, you are still on edge and do not feel safe until you are back in the vehicle.

More driving.

Around evening time, it starts raining and by nighttime, it's like buckets pouring down. Your clothing must be waterproof because the water just drips down.

12:00am.

Psshhhck. "Check it everybody, next gas pump's right outside creepy-town. Be on check while we shoot up."

It's the captain. The masks are linked with a built in communication system. It makes sense, but it startles you anyways.

Everyone turns to face out, and you quickly follow.

The outside world looks like a black hole.

Avery reaches over and clicks on the flashlight of your gun, but it only reflects off the rain. To the front of the vehicle, the headlights reveal the beginnings of a rundown town. What looks like mud is caked onto the buildings, and the windows are shattered. Trash litters the streets and there are other masses strewn across the ground that you cannot recognize.

That's a skeleton.

Your eyes are locked onto the gnarly mass. Shouts to your left make you focus back on your gun. Your heart is pounding. All you can do is stare through the sight of your gun, prepared to shoot at anything that moves. In your head, the image of the skeleton is burning. What had killed it? It was leaning up against a gate, with its fingers laced through the wires as if trying to pull itself to its feet.

You shake your head to get the image out. *Focus.*

Then you see it.

It's barely a shadow in the shadows, but something is slowly coming towards the truck. Your heart seizes up in your chest. And then several rat-a-tats sound and the thing jerks backwards at the spray of bullets.

Water drips down the screen of your mask.

Sweating. Breathing. Shaking. Do not look away from your gun to adjust your jacket.

To your right is more movement. You jerk your gun towards it and freeze. What is it? What *is* it?

It's a man. A freaking man is stumbling towards you in the pouring down rain.

Chapter 19

Your light shines perfectly on his disfigured face. Based on his clothes alone, you'd judge him to be homeless. He is missing a forearm. In its place, is a tan-ish bone and red, meaty flesh. His eyes are hazed over with a zoned-out look, and his lips are gone, revealing rotten, yellowed teeth.

POW.

The man's face explodes and he crumples to the ground. Of course, Avery is the one that shot him. Her gun is sweeping back and forth, looking for any more targets.

"Great, you've checked it, now start jamming." She says.

This is crazy that this is happening! It must be a dream. It *has* to be a dream.

No hesitation the next time you see one. At the first signs of their form emerging, you release a few bullets and it falls back into the darkness.

It locks up and stops firing.

"How does this stupid gun work?" You say out loud.

"Wait, you don't know how to jam a gig?"

Great. Stupid headsets.

"These guns aren't like the ones I've ever seen." You say.

The zombies just keep coming. Then someone on the intercom speaks.

"Cap, there are too many! When we done shooting up?"

"Only a few more gigs to go! Just hang on!" The captain replies and you feel your chest tighten. It is taking forever and the truck's completely surrounded, "We will never make it to the next check point if we don't fill up."

"Yeah, well it's either get eaten trying to fill up or run out of gas *almost* to the next checkpoint! Let's just tear!"

Better to run out of gas than get eaten here, in this mad creepy zombie town. Something clunks under the vehicle and then the engine starts. The truck lurches forward and into the town.

Eerie, flickering lights illuminate the streets, revealing tons of people huddled around. Some look less rotten than others, some even look perfectly normal, but they all have that zoned-out look in their eyes.

You hold your gun up, prepared to start firing, but none of them move. They just watch the truck zoom down the street. And then at the last possible second, they snap as if realizing they are being left behind. They screech and stumble towards the vehicle in a staggered run. Your heart leaps to your throat and you release bullets.

It is strange how they are able to perceive the truck and the people inside. They almost seem mad about it. And you almost think you hear an, *'I hate you!'* but it's probably just your mind playing tricks.

And then you're on the other side of the town, turning off the road and into the woods. On the road you are leaving, there sit rusting cars and zombies are banging on the inside of the windows. How did they get trapped inside of cars? One smashes his head through the glass and dives out, but the truck is already far off in the woods, too far for him to pursue.

Then it's all gone. The road, the cars, the village, the zombies.

Stunned. Sitting. Silent.

Who is speaking to you over the intercom? You don't really care. The guy says,

"You'd all be flat in minutes without all of us rips and without this fast moving piece of dig." He kicks the inside of the truck.

Then someone else laughs a quick, short huff. The captain again.

"We'd better hope this, 'piece of dig' gets us to the next gas pump or we'll be out there kissing their rotten eyeballs."

An involuntary groan escapes you and your head hangs in exhaustion. Avery. She's the only person you trust talking to right now. But it's still raining and whatever you say will be heard on the headset. So, you are alone. Alone, frightened, and shocked, with images of marred flesh and yellow eyes bouncing around in your head.

Chapter 20

You are standing on a rock in the mountains, viewing the horizon. How'd you get here? Doesn't matter. There's a strange noise coming from below your rock and you feel absolutely certain you must know what it is. But there's a sense of warning flashing in your mind. Disregard it. You have to know what that noise is.

So you slide off the rock and circle to the front.

Shoot. It's that man; the first one you saw coming towards the truck. Didn't he die? Yet here he is, hunched over something and gnawing at it with his bare mouth. It's a dead deer. Your stomach does flip-flops and just as you take a step back, he snaps his head towards you and smiles.

"I hate you!" He screams insanely and lunges at you.

Awake.

Whew, you are totally awake now, glancing around to make sure you are safe in the truck. Hands are clenched to fists, sweat making your entire body shake with queasiness.

Avery is there, tapping you. Inhale a sleepy breath and go to rub your eyes, but the mask blocks you out.

"How you checked, Trip?" Avery is saying. You still feel like you're in the dream, and cannot get the image of his psychotic eyes out of your mind.

"I'm not too sure." You sigh, "That was crazy."

"Any of it feel familiar?"

"No. This is not supposed to be happening. I should be home now." Is your explanation.

"Hmm." Avery responds. Before she can ask more questions, the nerdy guy comes over. You can see his glasses through the visor.

"I've been instructed to do rounds." He declares. The mask makes his voice sound emotionless and blank. He kind of pauses and looks at you before continuing, "You dug's doing alright?"

What the heck is a dug?

Avery quickly covers for your lack of reply,

"Yes, yes sir. Thank you," she glances at the patch on his shoulder, "Number Five."

The soldier stirs hesitantly.

"Alright." He says, "If you need anything, or have any questions, don't hesitate to ask." He then awkwardly steps away to move on to another group of people. Avery turns in her seat and smacks your arm.

"He's wearing glasses! I've heard about them but never checked one. Only City people can afford jagging like that." She exclaims.

"Oh." You say, "That guy seems weird. Like he knows something."

"Knows what?" Avery asks, surprised again.

"I don't know." You shrug, "Something about me, I guess."

"What could he possibly get about you that you don't?" She questions.

"I think he knows something about what's happening to me. He pays too much attention. He's probably a scientist or something."

Avery actually laughs at this and pats your back.

"You are such a trip, jag-face." She says.

"Well, if you're gonna keep pretending like you don't know what's going on; I have more questions."

"Oh, great." Avery becomes moody again, "My favorite part of each day."

"The zombies seemed mad at us. Like they hated us leaving."

"You what?"

"The zombies. They seemed angry."

"What's a zomvee?"

Ok. This is just getting ridiculous.

"You know, a person that's come back from the dead."

"You really are jagged."

"You know I'm just trying to understand things!" You argue, "What good am I to anyone if I don't know anything?"

"You're the one that just made it through a Krok fight without jamming up." She deflects.

"So you call them Kroks? What does that mean? Why aren't they called zombies?"

"I don't know what a zomvee is. And how do you not know what a Krok is? Haven't you spent your whole life shiving in this flat?"

"I don't know how to respond to that. You're the one that's pretending like busses and schools and cell phones don't exist!"

"You are so jagged." She says. It doesn't seem insulting this time, she actually looks sorry for you like she thinks you're insane. "Kroks are just people jammed up on dust. Krokodil mostly, but it's whatever they find."

"Krokodil; like drugs?"

"Yeah, that's what I flapped, isn't it?"

You gasp.

"So they aren't *dead*? I just killed actual people!?!"

Avery squints her eyes at you.

"You jammed up and flying?" She says, "Of course they're not dead, why would we jam up a bunch of flats? That would be a waste of gigs."

This is insanity.

"Okay, first of all; how are that many people using drugs? How did all of this happen so quickly? Did I miss something? Have I been in some sort of comma for a while and just woke up?"

"I don't get a dig about your life; why would you ask me something like that?"

Argh! This is so stupid!

"If they aren't dead, why aren't we helping them?"

Avery turns her head away and rests forward on her knees.

"Who gives a shot? You can tell yourself they're not flat, but they are to me. There's no hope for the rotten jags."

"That's just dumb. I don't agree. There has to be some way to help them; at least the ones that are still intact."

"Yeah," Avery laughs, "You wanna go into a shack full of jammed up trips and tell them to stop breathing, don't come crying when you're the one that's flat."

"What do you mean? Why can't they breathe?"

She glowers at you.

"You can take your mask off if you want." She says sarcastically.

"You mean to tell me that we can't breathe the air because of drugs? What, are they in the atmosphere now?"

"Yeah." She nods, "Everybody gets that, how do you not? The government jammed up the air eighty years ago and it's been this way since then; your momma never teach you this stuff?"

"What do you mean eighty years ago, is it some sort of science experiment gone wrong? Have they been doing this since the 1940s?"

"You don't flap a check. Why would I know anything about the 1940s? That was like, hundreds of years ago!"

"No, it was eighty years ago! You just said they put drugs in the air eighty years ago!"

"I think you're jammed up on dust, that's what I get."

You take this as a cue to shut up and so you do.

The rest of the day plays out pretty dull. Bathroom breaks, eating, sleeping, more eating, more bathrooms breaks. It is a good refresher from what you saw the night before.

You are just entering the deepest part of the night's sleep, when you awake to the feeling of the truck lugging to a stop. You vaguely hear the captain shouting, and everyone else is either stirring awake as well, or whispering to each other harshly.

Avery is sitting next to you, awake, and her eyes are fixed on the surrounding woods.

"What's going on?" You demand as you sit up and grab your gun. When Avery says nothing, you shove her, "Avery!" You shout and she shakes her head and looks at you, waking from her shock. You barely hear the words she speaks, as you already guessed it yourself.

"We ran out of gas."

Chapter 21

For the first few minutes, you all sit quietly with flashlights on, waiting for the captain to assess the situation. The engine shut off, and no one is speaking, so it is deathly quiet. No one really needs to speak though; there is nothing to say. So you all wait in the dark.

Then the captain stands from his position outside the truck, next to the gas tank, and slaps an oily rag over the rail.

"Alright," he begins, "Numbers Seven, Eight, and Nine; you're flipping out with a gas tank. Go shoot it up and bring it back. Pumps' about five miles southeast. Should take you around four hours." He tilts his head slightly when he says this last part, "Hurry back."

The three soldiers all stand and hop out of the vehicle. The tank the captain is talking about is kept under the vehicle. One of them bends down and you feel the truck lurch, and then the soldier is there again and he has in his hands a black plastic canister.

They jog off into the darkness.

It is quiet again.

Every now and then, something attached to the dashboard makes a scratchy beep. Why'd you never heard it until now? But then it was never so silent before.

It made it impossible for anyone to miss it. The roar. It is carried across the air, and sounds like it's pretty far away. Everyone jumps slightly and fingers their guns anxiously. Once the initial shock dies down, the captain jumps in the vehicle, marches to the back, and pulls the communication device from a hook. Its spiral cord is long and all tangled up, but he doesn't bother fixing it. Instead, he pushes a button on the top and it does another one of those scratchy squeals.

"Base Number Five, this is Captain Ben. Do you check?" He says. A moment later, the device bleeps and a voice comes on.

"Captain Ben, this is Base Number Five. We check. What's going on?"

You can't help but feel relief. The captain stirs and puts a hand on the dashboard for support.

"We are stranded five miles northwest of checkpoint..." he leans over to glance at some readings on a screen, "number 8368. If we do not contact you within four gams, be checked to send baggers."

"Checked. We'll be on the ready."

The captain then hangs up the device and climbs back out of the vehicle to stand guard. You lean over to Avery.

"Is it really that bad?" You question. Avery does not move.

"Doubt it," she replies, "they just like to be extra careful."

Done with the conversation. Your wristwatch says it's 1:15 in the morning.

Chapter 22

How long have you been sitting here? It's 3:30am now. You start and shake your head to wake up. It is almost time.

A few minutes later, something in the woods stirs and everyone becomes anxious. It's an animal, it has to be. But you have not seen one single animal this whole trip.

"Where are all the animals?" You question Avery, but the captain turns to the vehicle and points directly at you.

"Number Eighteen, flap up." He demands and you shut right up.

4:15 comes around and the soldiers still are not back. Then the base is on the com's system again.

"Captain Ben, this is Base 5. You still shiving?" It says. The captain jumps back into the vehicle to snatch the device and he replies,

"Base 5, this is Captain Ben. We check out. Our gassers are not back yet though. Should've taken them around four hours. If they're not back soon, we might have to send out another camp to check."

"Check it." The voice comes back, "Keep us posted."

Another noise sounds in the woods and the captain speaks one more time,

"Wait, I think they're here now."

As he is finishing his words, a burst of gunshots ring in the distance and everyone leaps to their feet. You already have your gun up and your head ducked to peer through the sight.

Oh, look at that. You are just like the others now.

The gunshots come in spurts and after a few moments, they stop entirely.

Silence.

"Number Seven," the captain is speaking through the headsets, "Do you check...? Number Eight? Nine?"

The captain has come to stand next to you, slightly crouched with his gun aimed into the darkness.

"Ferrell! Max!" He gives in to a shout, "Dan it Margo; what's going on!?!"

Then one of the other soldiers on the truck is speaking.

"Captain, incoming." He says.

"Is it ours?" The captain replies.

"Nope."

Chapter 23

Slowly, they emerge from the shadows.

Your body is shaking uncontrollably and you feel cold. Movement to your right. It's the captain, lifting the tops of the benches to reveal compartments underneath.

"Gig up. We've gotta fight through this one." He says and someone opens the bench on your side. It is full of handguns and machetes and bayonets.

Can you really fight them, knowing that they are not actually dead?

Guns begin firing.

You attach a bayonet to your gun, one maybe a few inches longer than the barrel, and then grab a handgun that is in a leg holster and clip it on as fast as you can. Your hands are trembling and you can't quite get it into place.

"Number Eighteen, hurry up we need you!" The captain yells.

Clack, clack, clack.

The plastic ticks as you try to fit the pieces together. Finally, it clips into place and you pull your gun up and face the Kroks.

There are so many.

For every one that falls, there is another to take its place and they are closing in on the truck.

Cha-chick. Bang. Cha-chick. Bang.

You begin releasing bullets. The Kroks snap, and sprint toward the vehicle.

For a moment, all you can see is their furious faces. Gleaming, sticky flesh. Rotting eyes. Yellow teeth.

The soldiers around you start climbing off the truck to fight the Kroks head on.

Then something snaps in *you*.

There is a rush of adrenaline and anger. You snatch a knife from the bench and tackle one of the Kroks, driving the knife into the base of his neck.

Now above him, staring down at his demented face, and he begins hacking and sputtering and his eyes are lolling around and twitching. The wound wasn't enough to kill him. Don't make him suffer. You pull your knife out and close your eyes to stab him somewhere unseen.

Agh! His body is spazzing beneath you! More stabbing. Still stabbing. He's stopped moving. But you're still stabbing because all you can think about is his contorting body. Get up before you see what you've done to him.

The rest of your camp has climbed from the protection of the truck and is fighting the Kroks on the ground, with brutality and fierceness.

Then something grabs you from behind, lifts you, and flings you into the side of the truck.

Chapter 24

Pain zips into your shoulder and neck. Stars cloud your vision. On the ground, staring up at the sky, wanting to die.

But those hideous creatures are still coming towards you. Reaching down with your good arm, you pull out the handgun and blast them in the head.

Gosh, it hurts so much. It's definitely not broken, but it feels impossible to move. It must be pulled out of socket. And your neck is shot; you can't look left too quick.

Onto your stomach and standing to your feet, but another Krok is there, screeching as he grabs you by the shoulders. Falling back against the truck. His teeth chomp at your face and spit flies onto the screen of your mask.

Can't reach for any weapons, and you dropped the handgun anyways, and he is so strong. Unnaturally strong.

A spray of blood covers your mask and the body slides off, falling at your feet. A hand lands on your shoulder.

"Come on!" It's some random soldier.

"I can't see!" You scream in a panic, trying to wipe off the blood but only smearing it around. Something else splashes in your face, probably water, and the blood sort of washes away.

Where's your handgun? There it is. There's no time to get it. Your arm hurts so bad. All you have is your shotgun-type gun. Blast them away, then.

Explosions and noises everywhere. Somewhere along the way, you find out that the barrel can twist around, becoming a machine gun. But don't machine guns need chains? This gun makes no sense.

Then you're out of bullets. Reach into your belt to load more.

You drop one, bend down, pick it up, and shove it in and rack your gun and aim.

BANG.

Blood spurts from the chest of the Krok and it jolts backwards and falls.

"Mind the truck! Jamming Kroks are attacking the truck!" The captain calls out.

The Kroks are at the vehicle, literally throwing their bodies into it, grabbing at pieces and ripping them off with inhuman strength.

Spraying bullets into them, explosions everywhere. Other people are targeting them too, but then there are the incoming. It is impossible to focus on one group.

You feel the Krok coming up before you see it and you turn and stab your gun into his chest, but he flails his arms around as if he doesn't even notice he's been impaled. You pull the trigger and he flies off the end at the impact, falling on the ground with his front all torn up.

Pain in your shoulder. The other one. There's a gash there, that goes right through both layers of clothing. It is all bloody. Great, now both your arms are wounded. How did he scratch you without you noticing?

Just start fighting again.

Then there are a lot less Kroks than there were before. And now there are none. Just like that, the last one dies and the battle dies with it.

Chapter 25

There are less people than there were before. Nine, not including yourself. Avery is alive, and the captain, and number Five, the others; Three, Twelve, Fifteen, Thirteen, One, and Four.

Ten freaking people. Out of nineteen.

The truck's been gutted. It's parts ripped and showing the inner makings.

"Alright, check it!" The captain yells. He's over there, wiping the blood off a deadly looking machete, "Get every gig we can carry. Kroks destroyed the jagging system, gotta walk to the next checkpoint. Who knows where the others are, but I doubt they're shiving after the dig we just went through."

"Where we headed, Cap?" Someone asks. Number Three. The captain turns to him.

"To the Tank. Our job is to get these cans there, and right now it's the closest thing to us. We'll be there in three days. Two; if we can catch a gig.."

"But will they let us in? I mean, by now we're nowhere near lizzed."

The captain has already hopped back in the truck and is examining the dashboard's damage.

"They've got a da-" he freezes in mid sentence and shoots a glance at the civilians as if reminding himself you are there, "a dan sanitizing station at the entrance. We'll be fine. Let's just hope this piece of dig com system still works so we can let them know we're coming."

Already, the soldiers are gathering weapons and supplies and so you go to help them. Anything that is possibly usable; pile next to the truck.

Your arm is actually not badly hurt, probably just bruised. After exercising it in the fight, it now only feels a bit sore. It's the scratch on your other arm that aches. Burns, really.

The soldiers pass out the remaining weapons so that everyone is pretty loaded. You still have the leg holster (retrieved your lost handgun), and added shoulder holsters under your jacket. Everyone has a machete and two guns with a bayonet on each. It seems a tad excessive and also inconvenient, but that fact that everyone else thinks they are not loaded enough means it's probably necessary.

The captain has recovered the communication system and contacted the City and you are all ready to go. Until the captain sees you examining your scratch.

"You checked there?" He calls you out. Are you not okay?

"Y-yes I'm fine." You reply. He tilts his head a little, probably to get a better view of your arm.

"Checks like you got a bad scratch. Krok wound?"

Quickening pulse. Failure to breathe. Dry mouth. Why are you suddenly so nervous? There's just so much tension in the air.

"I got a scratch from a Krok in the hustle. Are they contaminating?" Is it a stupid question? Who cares.

"The dan air is contaminated. You don't want to fly up that way. Sorry, kix; but it checks out you're too late already."

And then he lifts his gun and aims it right at your face.

Chapter 26

"Wait!"

What's happening? Avery is standing in between you, holding out her hands.

"It's very unlikely it's jammed! Why don't we just bag em' up?" Her voice sounds so hateful, "I know you dugs have meds for that junk." She continues, "Oh, but I forget that you only bag each other because that's all you shoot."

The captain racks his pistol and takes a step closer to Avery, placing the barrel right between her eyes.

"We lost five Rips today trying to get you to the City so you can live all happy in your fancy new Tanks. There are thousands of civ's living jagged while tens of us are dying every day. So yeah, of course I care more about my Rips than you. They're a gig these days."

"Check it," Avery bargains, "We're already wasting a gam. It's not worth the kill. Besides, now that we're on foot, we want as many cans as we can get." This last argument seems to dig into his skull. There is a moment of silence as everyone just watches the situation. Then the captain lowers his gun.

"Three! Get the med kit. I don't care if you mummify the dan kix, I'm not taking any chances with potential Kroks."

Air that you'd been holding escapes from your lungs in a sigh. And Avery turns to face you.

"You're welcome, Trip." She spits and walks away.

Number Three sits you down and has you uncover the scratched shoulder. Then he pulls out some sort of bottle and dumps the liquid on your wound. Fire. It literally feels like flames are eating up the skin. It hisses and froths and tingles go up and down your arm. Don't be weak. You bite down on your tongue to keep from crying out.

He then takes a gauze cloth and wipes away the liquid, digging into your wound even more to wipe away any lingering germs and nastiness. And then comes the needle and thread. He stitches you up with ugly black crisscrosses, and now you're like Frankenstein's monster. His last steps are to slather some sort of sticky substance on it and wrap gauze bandages around it, and then fasten some sort of rubbery strip that feels tight and uncomfortable.

Not even waiting for the soldier to finish, the captain yells again.

"Check it, let's tear out! Make sure you got all your gigs, don't leave anything precious behind."

Pull up your suit and slip on your jacket. The rubber bandage shows through the rip in your clothes.

And then you are leaving. No one even bothers to bury the fallen soldiers, or pile up the Kroks, or hide the truck. You all just start hiking through the woods, parallel to the dawning morning.

Chapter 27

The woods are quiet and dry. There is no lush green vegetation, it's all dirt and tan-ish colored leaves on the trees and dead foliage beneath. You don't think your group can get any louder than the heavy crunch of their footsteps and jostling of their clothing. And you're no exception. No one even seems like they are trying to be quiet.

Around mid-morning, you stumble on a campsite that seems lazily put together and is trashy and grungy. The group does a quick scan to make sure no one is there. You peek in a tent and see plastic bags packed full of substances.

Drugs.

Most are just white and powdery. So this is where those people came from. Camping out here, loaded with, 'provisions', getting high whenever. The captain clears the area and orders the move on.

A few miles later, the black canister shows up. It is still full of gas, and there is blood sprinkled on it and the surrounding ground. The captain orders the soldiers to search the area in a fifty-yard radius, and they return minutes later with nothing. Except for number One. He is the last to return, and comes running back with something in his hands. A mask.

This means one of the three soldiers is now wandering around without a mask.

The captain is turning in circles, searching the trees with a dead-eye expression.

"Let's keep flipping. If anyone checks anything, don't hesitate to either jam it or call for us to jam. Dan Rips have probably gone Krok."

Krok. Drugs. Rotting flesh.

There's hope for the soldier then, right? He's probably just off somewhere in a stupor, unable to comprehend what's happened to him. He could put on a mask until the drugs have worn off. But something is wrong. The soldiers are quiet and cautious, casting unsure glances at each other.

Everyone is on edge because of it and tries treading quieter from that point. But anytime a twig snaps or someone rustles the leaves, guns jerk in that direction. One time, an especially nervous dude tries shooting, but his gun only ticks with empty triggers since it detects no Kroks.

Then the inevitable happens.

Everyone is just beginning to relax, when a twig snaps to your left and you all turn to see him.

To the others, he's just a soldier.

To you, it's you're escort; Max.

Chapter 28

He stands a little higher than you on a sort of slope. His chest heaves quick, heavy breaths and his constricted eyes dart around anxiously. Face is flushed, drug intoxicated; he keeps twisting his head at odd angles as if he has an itch on his neck.

Everyone falls silent, waiting for the captain to make a decision. He is the first to step towards the intruder, and he holds a hand out as a signal to stand down.

The soldier still has his gun, but it trembles from his unsteady hands.

"Max..." The captain bargains, "What's going on, man?"

The soldier's eyes shift to the captain and flash with anger.

"You left me!" He spits, "You left us all flat!"

"Calm down, soldier. No one left anyone." The captain argues, "You aren't thinking straight."

The soldier just barely starts to raise his gun.

BANG.

The captain has already taken out his pistol and it's smoking. The soldier jolts and sort of staggers around a little as a dark red spot begins seeping on his chest. His face is odd, as if he's fighting to ignore some unheard voice. He shakes his head, and then looks up and charges at the captain with his hands outstretched like claws.

BANG.

Captain Ben shoots again, this time at the soldier's head and he jerks backwards and falls.

Horrified. Dumbfounded. Shocked.

Look away. Close your eyes. Why can't you just look away? It takes someone grabbing a fistful of your jacket and dragging you away from the scene for you to come back to your senses. Wasn't there anything that could have been done?

Chapter 29

Why did the captain select you to go scope with him? He says it's because he wants to keep an eye on you in case you go Krok. So basically, he wants to be able to kill you. If he's just joking, which he might be, it's not really funny. But you follow him to the edge of the forest, because he's your commander and he'll probably kill you anyways if you refuse.

You're on higher ground than the outside world, and in the distance is the skyline of a big city. It isn't far away at all. It's so close. You can see where the highways enter and where the first parallel streets run on the inside. Majority of the buildings are crumbling at the corners, and what vehicles you can see are fairly rusted.

"Is *that* the City?" You question and the captain laughs.

"You wish. Nah, that shack's more full of Kroks than a nest is full of bees." He kind of glances at you then, "Oh, forgot you probably don't know jack about bees."

Why would you *not* know what bees are? Probably has to do with the lack of animals.

"I take it that means there's a lot of Kroks there?" you question.

He raises the scope of his gun to his face and does not respond for a long time.

"Well," he finally says, "there usually are, but DU's don't really like light, so it's hard to tell exactly *where* they'd be at any gam." He squints and looks up at the sky to view the distant dark clouds that are on the far end of the city, "Right now there aren't any due to the sun. But I'd say we had a three hour gam before those clouds take over, take a check." He nods his head to your gun and you lift it.

The little circle surrounded by black is shaky and it's hard to focus on what you are looking at. But you shift in your laying position and steadily move it until you are staring into the streets.

They are trashed, but there's no sign of life. Or death...?

"So we're going in there?" You ask. He is staring through his sight at the city too. He then pulls away and stands to his feet.

"Yep. Come on."

The others are wearily waiting in a small clearing, and when you return, they all stand to attention.

"Alright," the Captain begins, "next shack is about two miles past the tree line. Didn't see much Krok so we should have about three hours to go in, hijack a gig and tear out. We'll just head straight down the main road and check it."

Chapter 30

It takes a whole hour to trek across the land and pass the outer rim of the city. The streets are relatively empty until you start getting closer to the high-rises. By then it is roughly 11:45 and the sky is now patchy with clouds. It looks like the storm is rolling in quicker than the captain anticipated. The sun is still shining, but there are random spots where the streets are in shadow.

Everyone moves quickly, skittering around corners and between cars. There are so many now, and some are smashed together in wrecks that nobody cleaned up. There are police cars and fire engines too.

Switching from looking for Kroks, to shuffling around pieces of trash. Some of it is blowing around due to the increasing amount of winds and one, a wrinkled poster, rolls right up onto your foot. Wait, what does it say?

'Caution: High Volumes of GID's! Do Not Proceed Without a Distillation Visor!'

Is that the name for the masks? Obviously. But what's a GID?

It's not a formal poster. It looks like someone scribbled the warning on a big piece of paper. They are all over the place.

On the walls, all sorts of psychedelic graffiti is sprayed. Some are just phrases scrawled across the buildings or in windows; Peace in after. Kill the Roses. No one wants a dime. Others are articulate masterpieces of depressed faces with cigarettes or blunts. One is especially freaky; it's a crocodile sprayed heavily with a red paint which had dripped on the bottom, making it look bloody.

Who made them?

It's quiet except for an unrecognizable noise that is growing louder the deeper you travel down the street.

The captain zig zags across the road, stopping at every van and checking them with some sort of device that beeps. He'll open the gas cap and slide in a long rubber stick with a small monitor on the end. When it beeps, and he pulls it out and moves on to another vehicle.

Closer now. Yep; it's definitely music. It's coming from a Thai restaurant and is that soft, pleasant oriental music.

"Right here!" The captain yells, now at a large van. He circles it to the driver's seat and smashes his machete into the window, shattering it to pieces. So much for treading quietly.

Someone taps you on the shoulder and motions for you to stand by a car with your gun raised. Everyone else is already stationed and so you lift your gun and stare down the alley branching off the main road.

There's a mass piled next to a dumpster. Is it human? Motion to the soldier next to you and point. He nods and starts inching forward with his barrel fixed on it.

Click.

You both heard the weird noise at the same time and glance down at his leg. A thin wire is stretched between the bumpers of the two vehicles and his shin is pressed into it. Warnings explode in your head.

Tripwire! Tripwire! Tripwire! They scream. *Stop him from moving, before it's too late!* But you're already too late. He casually pulls his leg back in curiosity, unwittingly releasing the mechanism.

Chapter 31

Noise everywhere.

Alarms, sirens, horns.

How are Kroks smart enough to set up such a contraption?

The wire is somehow connected to the vehicles on the street, and they are all going off.

Movement in every direction; Kroks emerge from places no one even knew they were hidden. Next to you, on both sides, Kroks awake in the cars and start smashing at the windows to get out. The mass of clothing next to the dumpster starts moving. You grab the arm of the soldier and pull him back. He was looking around in shock, but then he lifts his gun and releases a spray of bullets into the mass in the alley and it stills.

The noise cuts off moments after it begins, but you still hear it in your head. It doesn't matter if it's gone now; the people of the city are awake and they are coming.

Everyone backs together towards the captain.

Buildings, windows, vehicles, sewers; they are literally coming from everywhere. Like a wakened bees nest.

"Captain...?" A soldier questions. You tear your eyes away from the streets to look at the captain. He's leaned into the driver's seat with another contraption he's hooked up to the wires below the steering wheel.

"Come on... Come on!" He encourages himself.

Another soldier pulls out his handgun and blasts the head off a guy that comes from between the vehicles. He had no legs and was hobbling on the ground, but now he is blown back, just a torso with arms and a bloody spray on the concrete.

They keep coming.

"Captain!" The soldier screams again, and Captain Ben pauses to stand up. He lifts his gun to his head and starts shooting. Everyone follows.

None of the zombies are dying; they just kind of stop for a few seconds, twitch, and keep coming. Only a shot to the head brings them down.

Something weird happens though. There are a bunch of them coming from a building with glass showcase windows, and standing in one of those windows is a girl. She is zoned out like the rest, but she's not decaying. She looks so innocent and normal, except for her drugged-out eyes.

Man that's creepy. The soldier next to you takes a grenade from his jacket and pulls the pin.

Your eyes lock with the girls and for a moment, questioning and longing flickers in them as if she's asking you to help her.

The whole thing erupts in smoke and flames and the windows shatter. The soldier pulls you to the ground to shield you from the rain of glass that's coming down. The heat. The glass. The noise. There's no chance anything survived that was near it.

Then the captain is yelling again.

In your confused moments on the ground, you briefly see the others backing towards the vehicle with the captain in the driver's seat, pulling down on the stick shift. The van vibrates with life and the side door is slid open as the crew dives into it one by one.

Scrambling to your feet. Run for it. Wait, no. The other soldier is not with you.

You skid to a stop and turn back around for him; he's at your heels. A Krok is just leaping off the roof of a car to attack him. You raise your gun and release several bullets and it jerks back and away.

Number Five fighting his way up the street. There are several people attacking him at once, he doesn't have his gun, all he has is his machete. You and the other soldier shoot the zombies down and he breaks free. But then one comes from below a vehicle and snags his feet and he crashes to the ground.

The van starts driving away.

"No! Wait for us!" You shout, but engine roars as it takes off down the road.

Chapter 32

Ten seconds. It takes ten seconds for you to tackle the mass of rotting flesh and put a bullet through its head.

You turn to Number Five and help him to his feet.

"Come on, let's go!" Yells the other soldier, Number Three. Number Five runs a few yards down the road and snags his gun off the street. When he comes back, he grabs you by the arm and you follow Number Three into an alleyway. Put a bullet in anything that twitches or moves.

There aren't as many crazies this way and you start sneaking along down different streets. Number Three briefly speaks on his headset.

"Captain Ben, were heading southwest several blocks. Meet us within fifteen."

By, 'fifteen' he means fifteen minutes, but will the captain actually bother to stop and pick you up?

There are people you come across. They are different from the Kroks; they don't attack you, but it does not hinder you all from gunning them down in a panic.

Then the roars come.

You briefly glance back to see the mob of hideously furious people behind you.

Nope.

You run as fast as your legs will allow you to go.

Faces peer at you behind windows. The occasional slam of a door. None of these things matter more than survival. You are even outrunning the others only because they are actually bothering to shoot behind them.

All you can hear and see is the shrieks behind you and the streets before you. Your vision shakes with the intensity of your run.

On the main road again, there is another mob waiting you. Not so much waiting for *you* as they are throwing themselves at the van. Barely do you get there, when the van drives away. And with just cause too; if it stays any longer, it will be overcome by the mass. Number Five grabs your arm to pull you away before you're noticed.

You unite with Three and run away, back down the alley with no destination, knowing only one thing; you have all been left behind by the van.

Chapter 33

There's probably no need for the three of you to run so far, but none volunteer to stop. In your desperation to escape the Kroks, you find yourselves in an old part of the city, surrounded by apartments, factory buildings, and occasional cafés. The sky is mostly overshadowed with dark storm clouds, but somewhere the sun has broke through and is shining directly on your path, making the buildings look golden against the gray background.

You never officially stop running, just kind of slow enough to gather your wits and assess the situation.

How do you get out of here? Which way will lead you out? It's like you're trapped here. You'd be just as likely to find the way out if you were lost in the woods.

Itchiness, that feels like it's on the inside of your head, inexplicably fills you with rage and frustration. What if you don't have the constitution to handle this life? That you *will* actually become crazy? Surely, being locked away in some hospital room, without knowing anything is better than this. But nothing in the merciful heavens grants you such a wish. You remain in the center of an abandoned road, turning in circles, feeling the ugly, shabby apartment walls closing in on you.

"Hey! Jag-face!" Someone grabs your shoulder and steadies you, "You jammed up or something?"

Number Three stares at you through the mask.

"I can't do this!" You gasp, feeling a whoosh of blood return to its normal pace. You reach out and grab them by the arm, unable to stop the words from coming out, "I want to go home!"

He yanks his arm away and shakes it as if you contaminated him by touching it.

"What's wrong with them?" Number Five mutters.

"You jagged or something?" Three says to you, "Gonna become a NADo?"

He punches you in the face.

What!?! Dude!

"You feel better now?" He questions, "Check it or we'll jam you flat. Can't have you being a lug."

The punch helped.

"Three, go easy no the dug. It's just a civ." Number Five says.

"Who gives a shot. We have to figure out what to do next." Number Three replies.

Great. You're stuck with these guys.

"There is nothing to figure out; we have to get to the City." Is the response of Number Five.

"What are your names?" You demand. Three and Five exchange glances.

"Corporal Haydan Branston." Number Five says.

"I'm Private Brook Bailey." Says Number Three.

"Jay Jack." Is the name you give.

"Okay, Cap Danny," Says Brook to Haydan, "What's the trip?"

"We have to find means of communication and contact the entrance base to let them know we're coming." Haydan says as he turns and starts walking down the street, "There's a chance they might pick us up or drop a parachute."

The airplanes back at the facility. Why hadn't anyone thought it was smart to fly to the City? What if the reason makes it impossible for them to rescue you?

"And if they don't?" You're questioning eagerly.

"We will hot-wire a vehicle and drive as far as it will take us."

The area is quiet and less trashy, but still has a sinister look. Something is odd about it all.

Curtains. Why are there curtains on all the windows? Maybe it has to do with the Kroks disliking light. That must be the case, but the buildings back on the main street weren't covered. And the sirens – who set the trap? The zombies? Unlikely.

One curtain is pulled back slightly and there are two eyes peering down at you. They look scared and let the curtain fall drop back into place.

A quick scan of the area reveals others are watching you too.

"We're being watched." You call out.

"I know." Is Haydan's response. Barely does he say so, when there's a revving of vehicles. In moments, motorcyclists and old cars speed onto the road and surround you. The passengers are mostly youngish men. They look horrible and ragged, and they all have bandanas covering their faces.

The main thing, though, is that they all have weapons, and they are fixed on your group.

Chapter 34

Leading them is rough looking guy with sandy blonde hair. He climbs off his cycle, raises his rifle, and points it at Haydan's head.

"Don't fight." He warns, "We don't want to flat you. We only want to talk." He's from England. No denying that accent. It's Brook who replies,

"Why should we trust a bunch of Kroks with gigs?"

The guy's eyes avert to him and they look displeased.

"Well aren't you just a shot of Shine? We aren't DU's anymore than you are. Don't give us a jam and we'll let you flip. We only want *him*." He nods his head towards Haydan. Haydan is leading you to safety, you can't give him away!

"You can't have him." You blurt.

"Check it," he squints his eyes to emphasize his disbelief, "I just said we don't want trouble. You two can go free, we only want the Cap."

"You dugs must be from the Union." Brook stalls, "I've heard about you. Heard you jam up the government and the City."

The guy shoots another glare at the Private.

"Glad to know we're jagged enough to be flapped about. Now let us have the dug." Sweat is beading at his forehead and he looks nervous. Is he crazy, or is it something else? Maybe the more time is wasted, the closer the Kroks are getting.

"What are you going to do with him?" You bargain. His icy blue eyes dart to you.

"None of your jamming business." He spits.

"Actually," Brook steps towards him, "it *is* our business. The Cap is flipping us to the Tank and we can't shiv without him."

"Very well then." He looks between you all cautiously, then says over his shoulder, "Jag em' all."

Several burly dudes get off their motorcycles and approach your group with sacks. You cringe. What are they going to do with you? There's no choice, though. If you want to escape the Kroks, you have to willingly let them cover your head and shove you in the back of a van.

Chapter 35

BAM!

The doors to your left slam shut and you hear the roar of your captors driving off. The van flows with them. The back seats have been removed and you can feel the hooks were they once locked into place.

Someone's presence is on your right, and someone else sigh's to your left. Haydan and Brook.

"What do they want with you?" You venture to ask Haydan.

"Either information, or they want to use me for something." He says. He must have come to this conclusion because the leader referred to him as a Captain.

"Are you going to help them?"

A pause.

"Probably." He says cautiously, "The government isn't scared of the Union. They have nothing to hide, and these people are just annoying. My duty is to get you both to the City."

"Why didn't they take our gigs?" You change the subject.

"Every dug needs a gig in case of a Krok attack. Out here, anyone who is not DU is an ally, technically."

"What is a DU? Is it different from a Krok?"

"You're jagged right." Brook replies, "DU just mean's Drug User. Kroks fall under the category of DU, but DU's aren't necessarily Kroks. They could just be fliers."

"Like the people we shot in the streets?"

They both grow quiet.

"I'm not sure what they were. You never really know, until they're charging at you like psychopathic maniacs. So it's better to shoot and hope for the best." Is Haydan's explanation.

"Oh." Is all you say.

"A Krok is any DU who is jamming a narco or stimmer."

Like that makes sense. At least they are informative, though.

"I thought the government dosed everyone with drugs." You question, "So how are there people who aren't Kroks?"

"Some cans who have distillation visors still shoot up, just not on dust that makes you go insane or causes you to prematurely decay." Brook says.

"This is so screwed up." You conclude, earning a confused silence from the others. "So how are these people not Kroks then? I mean, they don't have masks."

Someone from the front yells back,

"You're about to find out!" He says it with a giggle. It's weird how happy he sounds. Maybe this group really is on drugs.

Chapter 36

Your captors pull you out of the van and guide you through a maze of hallways and staircases, only offering a few hushed words of directions. Several times, you stumble onto the first steps of a staircase only because they failed to warn. Neither Brook nor Haydan speak a word, if they are still there, and so when they shove you into a rickety metal seat, you have no idea what to expect.

Your guns are yanked from you, as well as your jacket. Then your hands are tied behind the backrest of the chair. When they pull the sack off your head, there is a moment where your eyes adjust. You are sat in between Haydan and Brook like on the van, and in front of you is the British guy.

His chair is turned away, but he sits facing you and he has in his hands a golden apple and a glinting knife. His bandana is pulled down and you can see that his features, though weathered, look kind. He's obviously some years older than all of you, and so Haydan and Brook are helpless to fight him.

He is not looking at any of you, but is cutting slices off the apple and slipping them into his mouth, munching thoughtfully. His rifle is rested against the wall behind him, and he has two shoulder holsters inside which are tucked handguns.

The room does not seem like it is in an apartment, since the walls and floor is made of cement and the door a heavy metal. The sun shines through a yellowed sheet hanging in the window, making the room look golden. It's sweltering without the cool jacket, and ghosts of dust float through the air.

The leader finally looks up.

"Take them off, then." He orders some guards that begin pulling off your masks.

What! No! Why would they do this? They won't even give you a choice; they're just *making* you go Krok!

"NO!" You scream, darting your head around to avoid the guard's hands, "No! Don't you jamming touch me!"

You realize you are the only one fighting the guards. Haydan and Brook calmly allow them to take their masks.

When your mask slides off, it scrapes your cheek as it goes. The reality of the stifling room hits you as you try not to breath.

Nope.

You can't hold it anymore and gasp for breath, inhaling the dusty air.

Are you getting lightheaded now? Or is it just the suffocating room?

The whole time, the Brit only watches with curiosity.

"You two." He points the blade at you and Brook "Don't jag a thing. You're just here for your dug same as me. I don't want to waste a gam dealing with your loud flappers." He points at Haydan, saying, "Now, we get that you're on a transit to the City, we checked you back on the main road with your camp, and we know you're a Tag. So, here is what we want.

"We want you to shoot something when you get to the Tank, yeah? It's not a bomb, but it will help us to get more about the Trunks and how to jam em'."

"What is it?" Haydan asks. The guy observes him with squinted eyes for a few moments.

"It's a one way speaker that lets us in on their little chats they have." He frowns and nods his head, "Small enough to go undetected, and it's easy to shoot."

"Okay." Haydan surprises him, "I'll do it. My government commissioned job is to get these civilians to safety. I don't care how or what I have to do to succeed."

The guy only stares at him suspiciously.

"So," he makes little circles in the air with the blade, "you don't care what you have to do in the sense that you'll agree to anything as long as it flips you out, well," he stands up from his chair like he is getting off a horse. Then he's behind you, grabbing your head and sliding his knife under your jaw, "I'm jagging this can to make sure you follow through."

What does that mean?

Haydan stirs in his seat, sending a series of loud creaks through the small room.

"I told you I would help; I have nothing to lose by it. I could so easily do it undetected, so it's not like I'm putting myself or them at risk."

"How do I get that you'll *actually* shoot this once you get there? If I just let you go based on your flapper, you'll get them to the Tank and then what? Fancy a walk in the shack?"

The knife is cold and sticky from its time with the apple, but it's the sharp edge against your thin skin that makes you tense.

Haydan tries to fight against his bands,

"Wait! Okay, no. No, just – just hold on!" He stammers.

"I've held on a long gam – I've been pretty jammed with your camp." The guy responds to Haydan's panic.

"Please, don't do this." Haydan begs, shaking his head and staring at the guy with pleading in his eyes.

"Yeah, but if I jag em' I'll be sure to get what I want" The guy replies, tightening his grip on you. Your hair is pulled at agonizing angles because of his leathery hands. The headache is already creeping through your skull.

Haydan wrinkles his brow.

"Why?"

"Well, I was going to jam you up with the speaker, but you insisted on bringing your dugs." The guy exclaims, digging the knife tighter and it's breaking through your skin. Freeze. Don't move. Don't even swallow.

"Check it," Haydan quickly speaks, "I'm already willing to do what you asked without a problem. But I will outright refuse if you don't let me take them without a scratch. You know as well as I do that the City will only examine us when we get there."

"How else am I going to be sure you follow through?" He pulls your head back so your neck is more exposed. He is staring down at you with a humored expression.

"Please, just give us one day and we'll figure something out." Haydan argues.

The Brit pauses.

"Check it." He says and releases you, "You've got one night. Otherwise we're gonna jag this kix with a recorder."

Chapter 37

The three of you are put in a locked room.

It's even hotter than the first one, and the sheet in the window is more like a thick, grey quilt. Brook paces around the room, murmuring words to himself. Haydan rubs his face as he sits with his bag against the wall.

"What does he mean by saying he's going to jag me with a recorder?" You ask. Brook hastily turns around and declares,

"Checks he's going to jam it into your leg. It's a painful procedure and can't be undone or else you'll be flat - it's a jammed thing to do!" He turns away and runs his fingers through his hair anxiously.

Ugh. It does not sound good.

"Why did he take our masks off, though? what good would it do for him? Won't the City not pick us up if we have any amount of drugs-"

"No!" Haydan interrupts you with annoyance, "The air is not shot up with drugs. The gov only jams four times a year and the rest the air is fine."

Woah.

"Are you serious?" You spit, "So this whole time we don't have to wear these dumb masks?"

"Don't be jagged." Brook says impatiently, "If you're checked without a mask, you'll be jammed flat. Takes too long of a gam to check for dust."

"Also the scheduled doses are classified and Civ's don't get when the next one will gam." Haydan explains.

"This is sick! When did all of this happen? How long have I been unconscious in that room?" You exclaim. Brook turns to look at you with a surprised expression.

"You hear that, Danny?" He questions.

'Yeah," says Haydan, "I already knew about it from the beginning. It's why I was tagged for this transit."

What?

Brook laughs and runs up to you, grabbing you by the shoulders and saying wildly,

"What was it like? Tell me; what was it like without Kroks and Drugs?"

"What are you talking about?" You say, "Shouldn't you know? Or are you also pretending like you don't know anything?"

Brook releases you to turn away and put his hands on his head.

"This is a trip!" He says, "I can't get I didn't check it before! Dug even flaps like a chief!"

"Flap it, Private!" Haydan snaps, "You'll confuse the dig out of em'."

"What are you talking about?" You press angrily at Haydan, "I know you know something - what is going on, what is happening to me?"

"Flap up, Danny!" Brook says, "No jagging this gam."

"Yeah, I check it." Haydan stirs uneasily and rubs a thumb across his jaw.

"My dad…" he stands to his feet, "My dad was one of the scientists who built the time machine that sent you to the future. *This* future. You're the first person to have travelled through time."

Chapter 38

Time travel? No. It's not possible.

But then, zombies weren't possible either.

Everything in the room grows distant as all sound drowns out. Your stomach clenches with sickness.

Brook is saying something to you, but you push him away, barely mumbling the words,

"Just let me be alone." Then you're in the corner, curled up in a fetal position with your arms closed around your head, with only a few words passing through consciousness.

Time travel. Home. Could you actually go home?

Chapter 39

"Wake up, love."

The Brit is standing above you. The room has dimmed, but he has a flashlight that he's flickering into your eyes. You squint and raise a hand to block it out.

"Good, you're done charging. Come on, then." He clicks it off and nods his head towards the door.

When he leaves the room, you sit up and rub your eyes. Brook and Haydan are over there sleeping. Based on the soft grey ebb of light coming from behind the curtain, it is early in the morning.

What does this guy want? Is he going to put you through the surgery anyways?

With one last glance at the soldiers, you scramble to your feet and leave the room, where the Brit waits with a guard. They both have a gun slung on each shoulder. When they start walking away, you shuffle after them.

"You aren't going to implant me with the recorder, are you?"

The Brit perks and glances back at you.

"No!" He says with surprise, "I'm going to show you something."

"How did you know where we were yesterday?"

"Jagging trip wire system always lets us know when someones here."

"So you're the ones who set it up?"

"Yeah." The corner of his mouth pulls back in a smile, "We've got some main areas rigged in case of Rips. The DU's all check it and they wait around for something to set it off. It's a jagged thing to do, I know; but it helps us to not have to risk sharing checks with the Kroks, you know? Here we are, then."

You stop in front of a staircase that leads up and he motions for you to go first.

"Ah, wait." He stops you and slides one of the guns off his shoulder and holds it out, "You'll need this."

At the top, is a hatch with a window and it opens into the dawning morning.

On a building that views a lot of the city. The air is damp and windy, and there are puddles littering the ground. Around the edges and surrounding buildings, are stationed guards who are pacing and looking out on the world below. When the guy joins you, you gasp,

"I didn't realize we went up so many flights yesterday."

He doesn't react very much, only looks around with a thoughtful face.

"You didn't. There are lifts."

... He means elevators.

"What's your name, then, little jag-face?" He asks.

"Jay."

He sticks a hand out for you to shake.

"I am Riley. Folks around here call me the General." He explains as you shake hands.

Why's he acting so friendly suddenly?

"What are we doing up here?" You ask.

"Yes, well; I want to show you something." He walks over to the edge. Down below, the streets are empty.

"What do you check?" He asks and you shake your head.

This is one of those trick questions where your answer will be wrong no matter what.

"Nothing." Is all you can think to say.

"Yes, well; why is that? I mean, get it; Kroks have a gam, but I doubt their jobs consist of bagging a bunch of heavy banger's."

"Does that mean bomb?" You ask and he laughs.

"You call them cars."

Oh.

"Don't you guys have them?"

"Yes and no. We jammed some random ones so as to go unchecked. Clearing the streets like this, would draw too much attention. City would jam us before we could take one sniff of Cobra."

Cobra? Is that another drug?

"This road is a favorite of the Trunks." He continues before you can ask, "They cleared it along with the northern highway. We stationed here to supervise them."

Why is he telling you all of this?

He starts walking along it with his hands folded behind his back.

"We have taken over factories, you know. A lot of our men are young, like you, but they are buds. With my help, we got how to jam them again." He looks back at you briefly, "I don't suppose you'd get what a factory is." He takes a deep breath and holds his hands up, "It's a-"

"I do know." You interrupt, saving yourself from the explanation he was about to go into, "I've explored some before. I sort of figured that they made things."

"Yes, well; we found a few, *searched* for a few that made gigs. Mostly jagged weapons and ammo, but we make them anyways. A jagged gig is better than no gig."

"Why are you telling me all this? I just want to go home - I don't care about all this."

He seems disappointed.

"Maybe you'll care when you see them."

He grabs you harshly by the arm and starts leading you over the rooftops.

Chapter 40

Riley's militia has built a network of walkways that stretch over streets and alleyways, making them easily accessible. You reach an end to the setup and stop by the edge to peer over.

Below is a camp. Blankets and sheets are stretched between the narrow alleyway as a makeshift roof, but there are still some holes where you can see in. There are around two-dozen people making their home under the canopy, sharing food and water, offering blankets, hugging and comforting each other. One girl in particular, has her arms wrapped around her knees and is sobbing. Chalky looking scabs litter her arms and a patch of skin is missing from her cheek.

Across from her, a fellow in a dark hoodie frantically sifts through a pile of belongings. His actions are hyperactive and desperate. He pulls out a packet and shakily pours its contents onto the palm of his hand and shoves it up his nose. He inhales and slumps against the wall with a dazed expression.

"Dug's are so quick to get that what is flapped is golden, they don't stop to check it and just search for the truth." Riley says, "It's why people like you get so jammed; they know they were jagged enough to follow along."

You tear your eyes away from the scene to look at him.

"What about people like Haydan? He knew about all this and did nothing."

Riley shrugs.

"What makes him different from you?" Is his sarcastic explanation.

"Why are you insulting me? I've never done anything mean to you - I just want to go home."

"Yeah, that's it - right there." He argues, "Your generation is so jammed up about being safe and comfortable that you don't jam a dig about anyone else."

Ooo, he's being such a jerk. Technically, he's even younger than you are, since you're form the past. So he has no right to insult you!

"You don't even know me!" You say, "So why are you saying all this?"

He steps closer to you and stares you in the eye.

"Because I want to challenge you to start thinking for yourself and not going along with everything you hear. *You* be the leader. *You* be the one that says no. *You* be the one that's too smart for all this."

"Okay, so what are you doing about it besides jamming up the government?"

"Ha," he laughs, "I used to be a doctor. Went to school in the Tank, found out the truth and couldn't allow myself to jam for something like that. So I used my skill to live out here and round up Shivs and … help *them*." He nods his head towards the alley, "We have a med center here that forces DU's to go through rehab. Now you tell me what the government is doing?"

Okay, the government is jamming up the air with drugs. So what? Aren't drugs good for people?

"But the government *is* helping people. They are rescuing people sane enough to live and are taking them to safety."

He clenches his jaw and stares at you hard.

"And yet the supposed, 'unsane' ones are left to rot."

"Why are you telling *me* all of this?" You ask. He winces and looks out on the horizon.

"I think you could convince your jags to help me."

Chapter 41

Riley sends you back into the room with Brook and Haydan. The door slams shut and clicks with a lock. The sun is out by now and the room glows with golden light.

Haydan and Brook stand when you enter and for a moment, you all stare at each other in silence.

"Are you checked?" Haydan asks hesitantly.

"Yes." You reply and then sigh, wiping your sweaty forehead. It feels hotter than it did yesterday. "His name is General Riley."

"What did he want?" Brook asks and you wince like Riley had done.

"It's... complicated. Right now I'm not even sure I want to help him. I mean, I do *want* to, but I want to get home and you," referring to Haydan, "you know how to do that, don't you?"

"Well, here's the problem." Haydan replies, "Time... time is concrete. At least, well. Let me put it this way; we know what's already happened in the past, and every second that ticks afterword becomes a guaranteed moment. Right now, as I speak, these moments are becoming solidified in time. So it's impossible to go back in time and change things, unless it's already happened."

"I'm lost." Brook exclaims and Haydan huffs and rubs his face.

"Check it. Let's just sit down."

Scrambling onto the ground and sitting with your knees up, while they sit down facing you. Brook seems already educated with what Haydan is saying, regardless of what he said.

"My dad spent his whole life studying time, and the possibility of time travel. What he found is that events, choices, and circumstances – in relation to time – are concrete. Let's say you choose to eat a piece of fruit. Based on who you are, your particular circumstances, and the events that affected your mood; you're decision to eat that fruit is guaranteed to happen even before it happens. Once it happens, it's in the past and will always be there.

"On a larger scale, events lead to events, but based on the people in the generation, their circumstances, their preferences, who came before them; those events are basically doomed to happen.

"Now, we know what's already happened, what we don't know is what *will* happen. That's just our perspective though. Let's pretend time looks like a line, with pictures of every event going forwards and back. If we were to look at all of time from an aerial point of view per-say, we would see every event and ever circumstance that led up to those events. But there is absolutely no way to change it. So what's happened, *has* happened, and what's going to happen *will* happen. Still with me?

"So, you came to the future, a future guaranteed to happen. The question now is; are you going to go back to the past? Well, before we try anything crazy, there are ways to see if you'll succeed."

"Like how?"

"Well, there are plenty of ways. Before 2020, time wasn't disturbed by time travel. Now that you have time travelled, there will be signs of your life events all over the place. For instance, is there a record of what happened to your family during the legalization of drugs? Are you, right now, certain that you want to go back and witness the fate of your family during the Accident? Were there people who were overly prepared for it because some jag warned them that it was going to happen? Is your 2020 returned-self still alive somewhere? If not, is there someone who knew that version of you? If none of those things are answerable, that would indicate that you stay here, in 2100."

"This is insane. How am I going to find that stuff out?" You inquire.

"The City." Haydan states, "Any information we might need would be archived there. And in any case, it's a central starting point."

"Can't I just try to get back and see what happens? Why waste time going to the City first?"

"Because, why risk trying to get to the machine if we aren't even sure you're going to make it? One way is a fifty-fifty waste of time, the other is not. If we find out you won't make it back, we will stay safe in the City."

"But... you said it was circumstantial. So, what if right *now* decides whether or not I make it? What if choosing to go to the City first is what determines that I will fail to get home?"

"Because it's science. It's not just something you can try out. You could cause serious damage to yourself that way. You have to first be sure that it already happened."

"Ok. Okay; so, now we have to decide how to get there." You resign.

Haydan scrunches his face and looks around the room.

"There's no way we're escaping here. They have our gigs. We won't survive without them."

"Let's just agree to help the dan guy." Brook suggests.

"Are you gonna volunteer to be jagged?" Haydan scolds him.

"Is there a way to swear loyalty to the Union?" You inquire and Brook laughs at you,

"You're jagged!" He exclaims, "He's not going to believe that."

"There has to be a way to convince him without being jagged." You argue. This whole conversation seems ridiculous that it's even happening.

"He's right." Haydan speaks up, "Riley is right about the jagging; there's no way we're going to sneak something into the City. They will confiscate everything once we get there."

"What if one of us swallows it?" You question. Haydan and Brook give you a look of horror.

"Dan, that's jammed up." Brook states.

"You live in a world full of insane people and guns and war - and you think it's jammed to swallow a recorder? How is that worse than getting it implanted in your leg? Surely, it's less painful."

"But won't it disintegrate in our yums?" Haydan replies.

Yums?

"Aren't you the son of a scientist, how do you not know how the human body works?"

"I'll do it." Brook states and Haydan shoots him a look of disbelief. "What?" He shrugs, "Kix's got a point. It's not completely jagged. Also, it's something the City's never checked before and won't get."

He stands without any further explanation and bangs on the door.

Chapter 42

It cracks open and there is a guard outside.

"Tell Riley we want to speak to him." He demands.

The door yanks open and Riley comes quickly inside and shuts it.

"Well? What did you decide?" He asks.

"These jags only care about themselves," Brook says, "so it looks like I'm the jag who's gonna carry the recorder."

Riley looks at you all with deep calculation for a moment.

"You are all just agreeing to the procedure?" He asks.

"You're jammed if you get I'm gonna let you touch me!" Brook snaps, "I'm gonna swallow the dan thing!"

Riley looks at him with disgust.

"That's the nastiest dig I ever got. Why would you suggest that?"

"It was this dug's idea." Brook shoves his thumb at you.

Riley looks at you and winces.

"You're jagged." He declares.

"I've heard that a lot lately." You reply.

"Check it," Haydan interjects, "we're agreeing to help you, just let us get this over with!"

Riley goes to the door and thumps his fist on it several times. When it opens, he motions for everyone to go out.

He doesn't give much time to rest, only food and water and a bit of fresh air on the roof. When he comes to get you, he is wearing different clothes; a grey thermal shirt and his shoulder holsters, with an assault rifle and an earpiece. His pants are military material and he has fingerless gloves on his hands.

"Come on then." He nods his head to the building and you all follow him back inside, where he takes you to a room stocked with weapons.

"Right then," he says, "in order for you to be bagged, you'll have to have all your gigs, no more no less."

In the middle of the room is a table on which is laid out all of the facility issued supplies. It's kind of depressing, having to put the mask back on. The others probably feel the same way, since they only hold their mask to the side and wait for further information from Riley.

"My com is only linked to my gig so I can get back. I would link it to yours, but the Trunks would detect the tapping and delay you're rescue to investigate.

"Now I know I made it seem like I'm in love with the Kroks, but only as far as my jam can reach. Don't hesitate to make em' flat. We're going to get you to the city airport, where you, Haydan, will contact the nearest base and tell them to pick you up."

Another soldier comes in and delivers something to Riley, who in turn gives it to Brook. It is a small device, no bigger than the tip of your finger.

"That's our recorder." He says as he goes to a wall hung with pistols and takes one off, "We control it from here so don't worry about jamming it, only shoot it in a hidden spot and leave it at that and go on with your merry lives." He pulls back the slide of his gun to check the chamber.

"Just in case you backcheck." He racks it and points it at Brook, "You've got five seconds to swallow the dan thing before I blast your face off."

Chapter 43

"Five."

Brook quickly opens his mouth and shoves the thing in.

"Woah - wait a minute he could choke!" You yell, holding out your hands.

"Three." Riley skips four in order to show he's not taking any hesitation. Brook struggles for a minute as he gags with his fingers in his mouth, trying to shove the thing down.

"Two!" Riley is growing impatient. Brooks face turns red as he tries to get it down his throat. He neck is bulging where the piece is lodged.

"Give him some water or something!" You yell. Brook opens his mouth and shoves his fingers in one last time, so deep his whole hand is almost in his mouth. His eyes display the pain he's in. He gags and doubles over for a moment. He pulls his hand out and rests forward on his knees, breathing heavily. He finally looks directly at you and declares,

"You are a straight up flier."

Relief.

"Well, that certainly was quicker than jamming you in the leg." He says as he tucks the gun into the back of his pants and shoves several cartridges in his pockets, "We're flipping out as soon as everyone's gigged."

Chapter 44

The journey to the bottom of the building is hectic. His people are hurrying around anxiously, and you meet a group that are loaded with weapons. The group leader stops to whisper something to Riley, who nods and pats the guys shoulder. The guy turns to his group.

"To the roof! Let's shoot!" He screams and they burst into a jog and Riley makes your group push against the wall to let them through.

"What's going on?" You ask and he glances at you once the soldiers are past.

"Their prepping for our journey through the streets." He says as he continues leading you through the hallways.

Is it really that bad outside?

Everything is quiet when you reach ground. It is a one-level parking garage, and Riley sneaks you to the entrance and stations on one side of the doorway while Haydan and Brook go to the other. The streets outside are completely empty, as before.

So why are his people so nervous? But then Riley points to a branching street, where the edge of someone peeks around the corner.

"Jagged things are waiting to jam us." He says and you know he means the city people.

"How are we gonna get across?" Haydan questions. Riley continues to look around the street.

"Just wait..." He says.

Vroom vrrrrrrr...

A distant engine revs and Riley bolts into action.

"Let's out!" He shouts and runs out into the street.

Guns fire all around. The moment you stepped out of cover, the Kroks exploded from their hidings places, like the day before. They come from all directions, but none get closer than ten feet before they are shot down.

The car comes around the corner and lurches to a stop and you dive into the back seats behind Haydan and Brook.

Riley is shooting back as he is running, and when he reaches the car he slides over the engine and gets in the passenger seat.

"Drive!" He shouts once he's inside. The driver presses on the gas, skidding the tires as it takes off down the road. You glance out your window to watch the Kroks being shot down.

CRACK!

A Krok slams into the glass next to your face and you let out a yelp.

"Oi!" Riley warns the driver, who then swerves to dodge the attack. Riley looks back at you.

"You alright, then?" He asks and you nod. The swerving of the vehicle makes you sick.

"How did they get we were flipping?" You demand. Riley winces.

"They always know because they check our prepping."

Despite the crack in the window, you look out again and see that you are now on a raised highway that is in a tight curve, arched above a large space of field below. Well, it could be a field, but there's no way to tell for sure because the ground is covered in camps.

Families, elderly, children; there are thousands littering the ground. What are they doing? Why are there so many?

"Wow." Haydan comments.

"Why don't they stay in apartments?" You ask.

"Not sure." Riley replies, ducking his head to look out the driver's window, "Could be a number of reasons. Apartments could be too jagged to stay in."

The view is blocked as the highway levels out and reveals an airport ahead. People are gathered around the gates, pressed up against the wires and reaching through with their haggard arms.

They want to escape. What do they think they can accomplish at the airport?

"Right," Riley says, "We don't have roofers here. We'll all have to go in, no use in separating. Head off to the com's tower first." He nods his head to the left field, where a tall tower stands. Shouldn't it be dead? But those red signal lights are still ebbing on and off at the top.

The vehicle is accelerating. Then the driver jerks the wheel to the left and you slam against the others as the car veers off the road and crashes through the gate.

The ground is uneven and the car shakes uncomfortably as it speeds across the field to the tower. When it stops, Haydan slides out and blasts open the door with his handgun. The speaker turns on in your mask and you grab it and crank up the volume so everyone can listen.

At first, there's only his breathing and footsteps, but then he lets out a yelp and retches. Riley snatches the mask from you to speak into it.

"Cap, what's it; are you alright?" He asks.

"Yep." Comes the quavering voice of Haydan, "Yeah I'm fine; just a couple of dead bodies."

While he works, you look across the field to the gate, where the Kroks are still fighting to get in. At any moment, it could collapse from the pressure. The chances of Riley and his driver making it to safety are slim. Why would he risk coming with you if he's such an important general in the Union?

"Communication Center 51109, this is the City Base, we are responding to your distress signal?" Someone calls over a speaker in the tower and everyone gathers in to listen.

"Yes! Yes." Haydan replies frantically, "This is Corporal Branston; we were separated from our group yesterday near checkpoint 8638."

Riley perks and scowls.

"Branston?" He murmurs to himself.

"We're at the international airport; can you pick us up on the runway?"

"We will send out a rescue team to you. Be there in 20, Corporal."

Sighs of relief.

Riley is pensive. He's surveying you suspiciously through the rearview mirror.

Haydan comes down the stairs and hops back in.

"Let's go!" He says and the driver takes off towards the airport.

Chapter 45

Riley has you all prepared for the arrival at the front doors. The driver follows the signs for passenger drop-off and you're there in seconds.

There will be Kroks inside, waiting for anyone to come in, so there's no point in trying for stealth. The moment the car stops and the engine dies, everyone climbs out and sprints for the doors.

Somewhere in these few moments, Riley calls on the driver and they both spring a load of bullets into the glass.

Stop! Glass is falling everywhere, and Kroks are coming from the darkness of the airport into the line of fire. You station in formation on the walkway, plowing down the Kroks as they come. But then the glass is cleared and your group continues to run forward into the building, despite the oncoming people.

Past the entryway.

Maybe there are signs to indicate where you are in America?

Hah. Yeah right. No time to consider something like that. Between fighting for dear life, all you see are the stereotypical flight destinations.

Newark. Chicago. Houston. Where are you?

"Alright, this way!" Haydan shouts as your group kills off the last remaining Kroks. Don't think about the gruesome bodies lying everywhere. Just follow him down the empty corridors and lobbies.

The place looks like something out of a horror film. Traces of blood and guts are sprayed along the walls, and you're not sure what it's from. Maybe other people had the same idea as your group, trying to find means of escape here.

Sliding through security checkpoints. Jumping at the alarms that go off. Guess you're wearing too much metal.

Haydan stops next to an, 'Employee Only' door and bursts through it.

"Woah!" He shouts. You had all piled in behind him, only to be met by a group of five or six Kroks. He raises his gun and shoots. "Go back!" He shouts over his shoulder and you all scramble to get out of the narrow hallway.

When you're free, you start running again, but you hear the jogging footsteps of the people behind you and their tortured screams are close.

You run through a darkened corridor that opens to a terminal, only to be met by more Kroks waking to the sound of your entry. They were sitting around in a daze, but they now perk and twitch and let out shrieks of anger.

"This way!" Riley. He's behind you, ushering you into a hallway like the one Haydan tried to use. Haydan and Brook are already gone, but Riley and his driver are reloading their guns. You go through without hesitation, but then realize the others aren't following and turn back to them.

"Come on!" You beckon, but Riley racks his gun and says,

"You have to go on alone. If the Trunks see you're with an unlizzed civ, they won't even drop down."

How are they going to make it out alive?

"GO!" He screams.

Chapter 46

Haydan and Brook wait for you around the corner, and soon the three of you are sneaking down the different vestibules. Haydan seems to know where he's going.

The silence is eerie compared to the main halls and your boots squeak against the floors every now and then. There are dead bodies lining the floors and blood sprayed on the walls. A lot of these corpses are paired with guns and some of them are even soldiers. Every corner or doorway sets you on edge and your finger itches to pull down on the trigger at the slightest noise.

You glance down at your clock. 8 minutes left.

Wham!

Something bursts through the door on the right, crashing into Haydan and Brook.

Kroks.

They come piling out of the door like a mound of ants and split in both directions, pushing you further from your group.

No choice. Run for it.

Chapter 47

Sweating. Gasping. Running.

The chase is a nightmare. On every corner, you push off the wall for momentum. You're winding through the hallways in an endless maze. A screech sounds, a hollow, rotten noise that shatters your bones. Aiming your gun back and firing aimlessly, hoping to hit something and yet too scared to slow down and look back.

This is it. You are probably going to die.

But... wait a second. You leap over a dead soldier.

Adrenaline kicks in and you break into a sprint, just enough to give you more space between you and the Kroks. Then when you round the next corner, you pounce on a body and frantically search through his gear.

YES! Dang it!

Your pulse is racing, but you grab the grenade, pull the pin, and toss it into the oncoming mob while bending down and covering your head.

BOOM!

Snap, that was so much louder than you anticipated. A rush of heat and pressure hits, but it's your ears. You can't hear anything. How did you get all the way over here?

You are farther down the hallway, laying on the ground on your back. The Kroks on the other end are blown to bits of fiery masses.

Dazed, you drag yourself to your feet and begin to stumble away. But where? The room tilts and spins and you're sitting on the ground again, willing it to stop shifting like jelly.

Someone charges around the corner ahead and you raise your gun to fire, but he holds out his hands.

Riley. What is he saying? He is yelling and pointing, but you can't understand him. He's all muffled. All you can hear is the ringing. You bow your head and put a hand on it, ebbing into unconsciousness, but he snatches your arm and starts taking you somewhere.

As he's practically dragging you down the hallways, your hearing starts to return, but your mind is still foggy, like you can't quite focus on anything.

Hallways. Dead Kroks. Guns. Staircase. Brook and Haydan. Someone sliding your mask on over your head.

"... Go on! Get out of here – you're out of time!" Riley's words come crashing into your ears along with a pounding headache. But you know he's right. Stumbling up the stairs to meet Brook and Haydan and heading out the door at the top into a bright light. Sunlight.

And a loud noise. A noise like thunder and horses. You can't hear anything again except the loud noise. A rushing wind is blowing all around.

"Come on, Jay!" Haydan shouts and behind him is a helicopter that's landed on the asphalt runway quite a few yards away. Brook has already climbed into it and Haydan is halfway, beckoning for you to come. You start stumbling towards it; knowing that it is your only chance of escape. You can't miss it.

Bam!

Something slams into you and knocks you to the ground. Your only instinct is to fight and you claw and scratch at it until you get a hold of your hand gun and put a bullet through its head.

Rolling over.

Haydan has run back for you and lifts you to your feet. The pilot is starting to lift off.

Why? Because more Kroks are following you out from the airport.

Charge for it.

Each footstep pulls you closer, but you're so heavy and confused and the wind does nothing to make it easier.

Haydan grabs you and shoves you up onto the helicopter while he jumps for the landing skid, clinging to it with all his might.

Next to you, Brook fires at the Kroks below as a medic grabs hold of Haydan's arms to pull him up.

Then you're all on the floor of the helicopter, in shock, dazed, and thirsty. Safe, and acutely aware of your injuries; your face is scorched, your shoulder throbs, and blood trickles down the screen of your mask.

"You checked?" Haydan comes on over the speaker.

Nope. But you sit up anyways at the motioning of the medic. The guy shines a flashlight in your eyes through the mask. He's eyeing the burns on your face with disgust and disbelief.

"Can't really give much help till we get to the City." He explains, "For now, just take some water. I'll jam it with some meds." He hooks a flask up to the straw on your mask and you slurp it up anxiously.

Then you're leaning over to look out the open side of the helicopter. Below is the city, growing smaller with every passing second. Kroks everywhere. Thousands of them. Swarming the streets. Like bees. Like the captain said.

Home. You just want to go home...

CPSIA information can be obtained
at www.ICGtesting.com
Printed in the USA
BVHW041451190619
551436BV00013B/797/P